# Horse Crazy Lily

## Other Books Available

The Lily Series

*Here's Lily!*

*Lily Robbins, M.D. (Medical Dabbler)*

*Lily and the Creep*

*Lily's Ultimate Party*

*Ask Lily*

*Lily the Rebel*

*Lights, Action, Lily!*

*Lily Rules!*

*Rough & Rugged Lily*

*Lily Speaks!*

*Horse Crazy Lily*

*Lily's Church Camp Adventure*

*Lily's in London?!*

*Lily's Passport to Paris*

Nonfiction

*The Beauty Book*

*The Body Book*

*The Buddy Book*

*The Best Bash Book*

*The Blurry Rules Book*

*The It's MY Life Book*

*The Creativity Book*

*The Uniquely Me Book*

*The Year 'Round Holiday Book*

*The Values & Virtues Book*

*The Fun-Finder Book*

*The Walk-the-Walk Book*

*NIV Young Women of Faith Bible*

the
Lily
series

# Horse Crazy Lily

# Nancy Rue

zonder**kidz**

**ZONDERVAN**.com/
**AUTHORTRACKER**
*follow your favorite authors*

The children's group of Zondervan

www.zonderkidz.com

*Horse Crazy Lily*
Copyright © 2003 by Women of Faith, Inc.

Requests for information should be addressed to:
Zonderkidz, Grand Rapids, Michigan 49530

**Library of Congress Cataloging-in-Publication Data**

Rue, Nancy N.
    Horse crazy Lily / Nancy Rue.
    p. cm. — (The Lily series) (Young Women of Faith Library)
    Summary: Twelve-year-old Lily finds herself questioning her faith when
    her newly adopted sister, Tessa, disrupts their home and intrudes on
    Lily's new-found love of horses, then has a serious accident just when
    she and Lily are beginning to get along.
    ISBN 0-310-70263-1 (pbk : alk. paper)
    1. Adoption — Fiction. 2. Family problems — Fiction. 3. Horses — Fiction. 4. Christian
    life — Fiction. I. Title. II. Young women of faith.
    PZ.R88515Hn 2003[Fic] — dc21
                                        2003000551

Published in association with the literary agency of Alive Communications, Inc., 7680 Goddard Street, Suite 200, Colorado Springs, CO 80920.
www.alivecommunications.com

*Editor: Barbara J. Scott*
*Interior design: Amy Langeler*
*Cover design: Jody Langley*

*Printed in the United States of America*

07 08 09 10 11 12 • 19 18 17 16 15 14

**H**ey, Lily—you comin' or what?"

Lily Robbins glared into the mirror she was standing in front of. She was looking at her own redheaded self, but the glare was intended for her seventeen-year-old brother, Art. He was two floors down and probably tossing his keys from one hand to the other.

"Like he has so much to do on a Saturday afternoon," Lily said to the mirror.

But he *had* agreed to drive her out to Suzy's birthday party.

With a sigh, she untangled her way-long-for-a-twelve-year-old legs and got to the door, where she poked her curly head out and yelled back, "Don't have a cow! I'll be right down."

"Define 'right down,'" Art yelled back.

"Two minutes."

"I'm pulling out of the driveway in exactly two minutes."

Lily scrambled to the closet and dragged out the boots she'd cleaned up for Suzy's party. They brought on a grin. What a great idea Suzy had come up with for her birthday—an afternoon of horseback riding for her and all the Girlz—Lily, Zooey, Reni, and

Kresha. Lily had never been on a horse, though she'd always thought it sounded way cool. She felt like this was as much a present for her as for Suzy.

Lily glanced at her watch and then whipped her mane of curls around, looking for the gift she'd taken a half hour to wrap. She had put it right on the bed—and it should be easy to spot.

Since she'd moved into her new room up here in the attic a week ago, she hadn't had a chance to decorate—what her mother referred to as "cluttering up the place." The only things currently cluttering it were her stuffed animals. She could barely function without them, especially the giant panda, China, who she leaned against during her talking-to-God time every night—with Otto by her side, of course.

"Otto!" Lily said.

She heard him grunt from under the bed, and she dove for it.

"Tell me you don't have Suzy's present!" she said as she lifted up the dust ruffle.

Otto, her little gray mutt, blinked at her through the darkness.

"You do—you are *so* evil!"

Lily made a snatch for the blue-covered package and managed to get hold of the ribbon. While Otto tugged one way, she yanked the other and pulled dog and gift out into daylight. Otto's scruffy top hair stood up on end.

"I'm lee-ving—" Art called from below.

"Don't! I'm coming!" Lily cried. Grabbing onto the gift—and dangling Otto in midair in the process—she grabbed her denim jacket with her free hand and tore down both flights of stairs. Otto growled and snarled the whole way, but he didn't loosen his little jaws of steel, in spite of Lily's steady stream of "Drop it, you little demon seed! I spent my whole last week's allowance on that!"

Art, arms folded, was waiting at the bottom of the stairs.

"Grab him, Art," Lily said. "Make him let go."

"You gotta be kidding," Art said. He took a step backward. "I'm not touching that dog. He'll bite my hand off."

"What in the world—" Mom said. She appeared out of the dining room, dust rag in one hand, can of furniture polish in the other. Her mouth twitched—in that way it did instead of going into a whole smile. "Otto," she said in her crisp coach's voice. "Drop it."

Otto, of course, didn't—at least not until Mom sprayed some polish into the air above her head. Otto let go of the present and, tucking his tail between his scrawny legs, disappeared up the stairs. He didn't like spray cans.

"Can we *go* now?" Art said.

"Have fun," Mom said. "And, Lil—don't make any plans to spend the night with anybody tonight. You know tomorrow is a big day."

Lily nodded as she ran toward Art's Subaru—nicknamed Ruby Sue. She managed to slide in before Art got it into gear.

"It's that place over in Columbus, right?" Art said.

"Uh-huh."

"Could she have picked a place farther away?"

"It's the only riding stables in South Jersey, I think," Lily said.

"Tha-at's an exaggeration." Art had picked up a new habit of dragging out his words in a bored voice. Lily thought it must be some cool thing musicians did.

"So—what do you think this Tessa chick is going to be like?" he said with a snicker. "Her mother must have really had it in for her to give her a name like Tessa. What's thaaat about?"

Lily rolled her eyes in his direction. "Her mother probably *did* have it in for her, or she wouldn't have been in all those foster homes.

7

And we're not supposed to talk about all the stuff that's happened to her unless she brings it up, remember?"

"Like I'm going to forget. We heard it about a dozen times."

Lily had to agree — he was right about that. Ever since Mom and Dad had found out that the adoption agency had a child for them, they'd been holding family meetings to talk about Tessa, who was about to become their nine-year-old sister.

"She's had a rough time," Dad had explained. "She hasn't had any of the things you kids have had, including love or security or a family."

Mom was a little more direct: "You can't be doing your brother-and-sister routine while she's getting adjusted. No teasing — no kicking under the table — am I clear?"

"Have you noticed how different they are lately when they talk about her?" Art said now. "Now that they've actually met her?"

"No," Lily said. "Well — I did notice that Mom's cleaning the entire house with a toothbrush to get ready for her. You think Tessa's a neat freak?"

Art shook his head. "I saw a list of child psychologists on Dad's desk."

"Don't they send, like, mental patients to them?"

"Nah — half the kids I know are in therapy," Art said. "Whatever the chick's got going on, it's probably not that big a deal. I think Mom and Dad are freakin' a little."

The rest of the way to the stables, Lily forgot about horses and thought about Tessa. The Robbinses had known for a while that they were going to adopt a child, and Lily had been all over it — another girl to help her survive two brothers. She'd gotten excited about fixing up her old room for Tessa, but Mom had said they should just paint it white and let her decorate it how she wanted to, since she'd never had her own room before.

When Mom and Dad had come back from meeting her, Lily had gone to Mom with a list of possible sister activities they could do together. Mom had twisted her mouth a little and then said, "I know how you are, Lil—everything 950 percent—but, hon, you can't take Tessa on as your latest thing. Don't start reading child psychology books—"

"Mom, I'm so over trying to find my thing—"

"Good—then let's just let her get settled in and get to know her."

So Lily had been forced to put the whole thing in the back of her mind, behind math homework and Shakespeare Club and, of course, Girlz Only Group. She'd prayed for Tessa every night, but that was about all. Until now.

*What if she's in a gang or something?* she thought. *Is she gonna get off the plane tomorrow with a tattoo?*

"So is this it?" Art said. "Double H Stables." He snickered again. "Now thaaat's original."

"Herbert Hajek, Owner," Lily read from the plank that hung under the Double H logo on the gate that Art had pulled up to. "Of *course* it's going to be Double H. What else would they call it?"

Art raised an eyebrow in the direction of the tiny stables tucked between two maple trees. "Don't get your hopes up, Lil," he said. "I don't think this guy raises thoroughbreds."

"Reni's mom's bringing me home," Lily said as she climbed out of Ruby Sue. Which was good, because she'd had about enough of Art making everything sound worse than it was.

She forgot about Art—and Tessa—the minute Zooey, Kresha, Suzy, and Reni burst out of the stables, all wearing jeans and boots and bandanas tied to various places.

"This is going to be the *best*!" Zooey said as she tugged at Lily's arm. "We each get to ride our own horse and—"

"I get the wery strong horse!" Kresha said. Lily knew she was excited because her Croatian accent was slipping in. W's replaced v's when that happened.

Reni grabbed Lily's hand—the one Zooey *wasn't* wringing out like a dishrag—and tugged her toward the stables. She didn't have to say anything. Best friends, Lily had discovered, could communicate without words. Reni's chocolate-brown eyes, dancing in the glow of her matching-brown face, said that for once Zooey wasn't exaggerating. It was going to be awesome.

Lily let them usher her into the stables. "Awesome" didn't even begin to describe what she saw when they finally let go of her and let her look around.

It was dim inside, but even in the half-light she could tell the wooden floors were swept clean. The sun that crept in from the open doors on the other end brought eight stalls into view, four on either side of the wide hallway, each with the top half of its door open.

*I bet that's where you prop yourself up to give the horses apples and sugar cubes and stuff,* Lily thought. The smell was a mixture of hay and leather and—okay, maybe the *faint* odor of horse poop. But nothing had ever smelled as good.

"You girlies ready to ride?" said a voice from the open doorway.

Lily could make out only a silhouette as the Girlz all ran out to him. What she found in the sunlight was a man not much taller than her own five-foot-five—tall for a seventh grader but not for a man who had shoulders that looked like a set of football pads. She decided he'd be a lot taller if he weren't quite so bow-legged.

"I'll take that as a yes," the man said as the Girlz swarmed around him. He was wearing a blue bandana, tied tightly around his head so that he slightly resembled a cue ball with bright eyes. Lily didn't have a chance to see what color they were before he planted a battered hat onto his head and pulled the brim down almost to his nose.

"This is Herbie," Zooey said, giggling like a piccolo.

Herbie nodded at Lily and then at the line of horses that waited patiently along the wide dirt path the Girlz were standing on.

"First thing, Georgie and I will get you girlies up in those saddles," he said. His voice was as clipped and snappy as any other South Jersey accent Lily had ever heard. *That's funny,* she thought. *I expected him to talk like he was from Texas or something.*

That didn't make the idea of climbing up into one of those saddles any less exciting—or any less scary.

As Herbie showed Suzy how to put one foot in the stirrup and hoist herself up so she could swing the other leg over the saddle, Reni pointed to a horse the color of a brownie with a crooked white marking on his face that was shaped just like milk pouring out of a pitcher.

"This one's Big Jake," Reni said. "He's yours." Her voice took on a hint of envy. "I think he's the biggest one of all."

Lily agreed, but she couldn't nod her head. She'd never been this close to a horse before, and she'd never known they were quite this big. She had to look up to see under his neck, which he was now tossing around like he was impatient to get this party started.

Lily stood staring at him while the rest of the Girlz swung up into their saddles. Her mouth was starting to go dry.

*Maybe this wasn't such a good idea,* she thought, trying to lick her lips. *This is a big animal. I don't know what to do with something like this—yikes!*

"Your turn, girlie," Herbie said. He nodded at the stirrup. "Put your left foot right in there."

Lily felt a long pang of fear go through her—but she managed to stick her right foot into the stirrup. Herbie shook his head.

"Oh, sorry!" Lily said. "I always get right and left mixed up—" Actually, she never did, but right now her thoughts were like a herd of terrified ants.

When she finally fumbled her way into the saddle, her long right leg flailing the air for one endless, embarrassing moment before her foot found the other stirrup, Herbie said, "All right, girlies. We're all going to be together so I'll be watching your horses, but there are a few things you need to know."

*Yeah,* Lily thought. *Like how to get down!* She leaned over to look at the ground. The height was dizzying.

*What if I fall?* Lily thought. *I could break a leg! Or my neck!*

"That's all you need to know, " Herbie said. He started off toward the one empty-saddled horse on the path and then stopped. "Oh, one more thing—if you have any trouble with your horse, just say—in a calm voice, now—'I have a situation.' " He tipped his head back to look up at them. "You girlies ready to ride?"

He was answered with an assortment of yeses and giggles. But Lily didn't join in. She wanted to shout right now—"I have a situation! I don't want to go!"

But Big Jake threw his head back and shook his stringy mane and blew air out of his nostrils. *He* obviously *did.*

No sooner had the line of horses begun to move—one steed's nose buried in the tail of the one in front of it—than Big Jake tossed his head once more. And then he took off—ahead of the others—with Lily hanging on.

She screamed for all she was worth, "I have a situation!"

Chapter 2

The situation got worse by the second. As Big Jake lowered his head and went straight for a stand of maples, Lily clung to the handle on the front of the saddle. But it wasn't much to hold on to, especially when with every step Big Jake took, Lily's hind parts left the saddle, only to slam back down in a painful slap and then jolt up again. After three of those bounces, Lily flattened herself against Big Jake's neck. In that position, the handle on the saddle dug into her belly, but at least she wasn't being thrown up and down like a rag doll.

Lily grabbed around for something else to hang on to, and her hands found a fistful of Jake's mane on one side and a leather strap on the other. She got a death grip on both and cocked her head up so she could see where they were going.

Bad move. There was a tree limb straight ahead, ready to smack her right in the forehead. Big Jake lowered his head some more, and Lily let hers go down with him. The shadows of tree limbs dappled them from all around, so Lily didn't dare look up again. It was all she could do to hold on anyway. Sliding from side to side, she squeezed her eyes shut to try to block out the vision of herself hanging upside down underneath Big Jake as he plunged toward wherever it was he was so dead set on going.

Jake took a sudden veer off to the left, and Lily felt herself slipping, so she clamped her knees into the horse's sides to keep herself from going down. That helped her stay in place, but Big Jake seemed to like that—and ran even faster. Lily was sure if she raised up so much as an inch, she'd be beheaded.

It wasn't until Big Jake cleared the trees that Lily chanced a peek. Directly in front of them was the creek, ribboning its shiny way along at the bottom of a five-foot drop.

Lily had just opened her mouth to scream again when there was another sound—the pounding of a second set of hoof beats behind her, and then a shout.

"Pull the reins to the left, girlie!" a Jersey voice was calling. "Pull them hard and to the left—and don't stop pulling!"

Lily looked around wildly. Reins? Did she have those?

With Big Jake gaining on the creek, there was no time to get a definition. Lily just yanked what was currently in her hand to the left. Big Jake pulled his head sideways with a jerk, and Lily gave a squeal and started to let go.

"Keep pulling!" she could hear Herbie shouting beside her. "Hard to the left! Grab the other rein!"

His horse was out in front of hers now, and he seemed to be stopping.

*I'll run over you!* Lily wanted to scream.

But Big Jake was finally turning himself to the left—and to the left—and to the left—so that suddenly he—and Lily—were moving in a tight circle.

"That's it!" Herbie shouted. "Keep pulling to the left, hard as you can!"

It was only then that Lily realized she was the one pulling Big Jake into a circle. Above the din of Herbie's shouting and Jake's hooves clomping in the dirt, she could hear Jake protesting with a snort. But he was slowing down.

When he came to a reluctant stop, head tossing and hooves pawing, he was right in front of Herbie. And Lily was still on him.

She dropped what she now knew were the reins so she could cover her face with her hands, but Herbie snatched them up and stuck them back into her hands.

"Keep him under control, girlie," Herbie said. "Let him know who's boss."

*"He's* boss!" Lily cried.

"Don't pick your reins up," Herbie said. "Just hold them right in front of you and tell him, 'Whoa, Jake.'"

Lily felt like an idiot, but she said "Whoa, Jake." She would have said anything to avoid another flight for the creek.

Jake blew air out of his nostrils again, but he didn't move, except to stomp a little. Lily gave him another "Whoa, Jake," just to be on the safe side, and he stopped.

Herbie chuckled. "Looks to me like you're the boss now, girlie."

"I'm so sorry," Lily said. "I don't know what I did wrong—he just took off—"

Jake took a few steps forward. Lily jerked back on the reins. He settled down again.

"You can't be talking with your hands when you're holding the reins," Herbie said, grinning. "That will be the one hurdle you'll have to overcome in riding."

"If I ever get on a horse again!" Lily said.

Herbie jerked his chin up and down. "Just pick up the reins slowly," he said, "and kick your heels just gently against his sides."

"I'll hurt him!" Lily said.

"You're not going to hurt the horse. Just a little kick and pick up the reins."

"What's going to happen?" Lily said, still keeping the reins so flat against the saddle they were about to become joined.

"The horse is going to walk forward."

"Oh," Lily said. She looked at Herbie, whose bright eyes were smiling at her from under the brim of the hat that was wearing him. "You're gonna be right here?"

"Right here," he said.

Lily took a deep breath and slowly lifted the reins. "Okay, Jake," she said. "You heard that. We're going to walk — not run."

Then with another breath that she didn't let out, Lily bounced her heels against the big horse's sides. Like a miracle, he moved forward, placing his hooves politely one in front of the other and bobbing his head up and down with each step.

"Yikes!" Lily said. "I'm riding a horse!"

"You've been riding a horse ever since you got on," Herbie said, his horse rocking lazily beside hers as they moved toward the stables. "She's a natural. Isn't she, Jiminy?" He gave his horse's black mane a tousle with his fingers.

"Nuh-uh!" Lily said. "I didn't even know what a rein was!"

She cringed a little, waiting for the teacher question: Where were you when I was explaining all that? But Herbie was shaking his head.

"Most people would have fallen off," he said. "You used your natural instincts to keep yourself on." He chuckled. "Only thing was, you

were giving him the signals to go even faster. Jake's a good boy —
he'll do whatever you tell him."

"*I* was telling him to go faster?"

"The point is, you have a natural seat on a horse. A few more lessons, and you'll be on your way to becoming a fine horsewoman."

"Me?" Lily said. "But where would I get lessons?"

"I give them," Herbie said. "Hello, girlies!"

He stopped beside the line of Girlz, who were still mounted and
staring open-mouthed at Lily.

"You are okay, Lee-lee?" Kresha said.

"She's perfect, this girl," Herbie said.

Zooey's gray eyes were the size of wagon wheels. "Weren't you
scared, Lily? I'd have been so scared. I thought you were going to be
killed."

Herbie laughed his deep chuckle. "We haven't had anybody die
here yet," he said.

Suzy gave a nervous giggle. "Can we still ride?" she said.

"That's what we came out here to do, isn't it?" Herbie nodded his
head toward Suzy's horse. "Let me just get in front of you, girlie, and
we'll be on our way."

"Should Lily still be in the back?" Reni said. "What if her horse
gets away again?"

"Don't you have another horse?" Zooey said. "Maybe a slower
one?"

Herbie continued to make his way to the front of the line. When
he got there, he looked over his shoulder. "Girlies, Lily is going to be
fine," he said. Then he tipped his hat up with one finger, winked at
Lily, and turned back around.

"Head 'em up," he said. "Move 'em out!"

After Lily's and Big Jake's headlong hurl for the creek, the ride they took for the next hour was pretty tame for Lily, but that was okay. She rocked along on a now docile Big Jake, grinning at his refusal to put his nose anywhere near Reni's horse's tail.

They held back a little, Jake and Lily. While the rest of the Girlz were squealing and giggling Lily was already planning.

*If I'm a natural on a horse, then this is what I'm supposed to be doing! Maybe I should have been doing this all along—but that's okay. I can start today. Okay—first I take lessons. It can't be that expensive if I take them from Herbie. It's not like this is some ritzy place—*

Another idea struck her, and she did a quick calculation on her fingers. That jerked the reins a little, and Big Jake shook his head. She was certain he was trying to look back at her with a what's-going-on-Lil? look in his eye.

*It's only a month 'til my birthday. That should give Mom and Dad time to find me a horse. I won't even ask for a party or anything else for the whole year.*

"No offense to you, Jake," she said. "You're a great horse and everything, and I can learn on you. That way I'll be doing jumps and stuff by the time I get my own."

*Maybe I could get a job teaching some lessons to help pay for my horse's food,* Lily thought. *I mean, when I'm not being in horse shows and stuff. Wonder what they wear at those?*

By the time they returned to the stables, Lily had so many ideas that she could have skipped cake and presents to get home and start things rolling. But Suzy's mom had everything set up on a picnic table that was still within smelling distance of the stables. Lily looked back to see if she could get another glimpse of Big Jake before she sat down. Herbie was just leading him to his stall. He waved. She was sure Jake gave her a longing gaze.

Mrs. Wheeler was passing out cake when Lily saw Ruby Sue pulling into the driveway.

"I thought you were riding home with me," Reni said.

Lily watched Art get out of the car and wave her over. When she got halfway to him, he said, "Get your stuff. You have to come home now."

Lily's throat caught. Art looked pretty serious. "What's wrong?" she said.

"Tessa's already here," he said. "Get your stuff."

Everybody looked disappointed as Lily went back to grab her jacket and toss out a quick explanation. "Happy birthday, Suzy," she said, and then tore for the car.

"What happened?" she said to Art as she climbed into Ruby Sue.

"Some kind of snag. We went to get her right when I got back from bringing you."

Lily looked curiously at Art. "You look kinda freaked out."

He slid her a sideways glance. "Take everything Mom and Dad have said about Tessa—no social skills, no manners, all that stuff—"

"Yeah—"

"Then multiply it by about a hundred." Art gave her a full-on look. "That's our new sister."

Suddenly Lily wanted Ruby Sue to break down so it would take hours to get back to Burlington. All traces of horse ideas were gone, replaced by visions of a sister a hundred times worse than anyone she could think of—worse than Shad Shifferdecker, who wore the seat of his pants practically down to his calves and had been pointing out every flaw she had since the fourth grade.

"Tessa can't be that bad," Lily said as they passed the City of Burlington sign. "We saw her picture. She looked okay."

"She got a haircut since then."

"So what's wrong with a haircut?"

"Juuuust get ready," Art said.

"How am I supposed to get ready when I don't know what I'm getting ready for?"

Art didn't answer. Lily settled into a nervous silence and looked out the window without seeing anything.

*No wonder she didn't answer any of the letters I wrote her,* Lily thought. *And Mom said she didn't say anything about the bubble bath I sent for her when she and Dad went to see her. I bet she did say something. Maybe she said it was stupid.*

"They should have told us," she said.

"I don't think they knew, Lil," Art said. "I think they're as blown away as we are."

They didn't say anything else until they pulled into the driveway. But somebody else was definitely saying something — screaming it, was more like it — somewhere in the direction of the backyard.

Art took the front steps in one long-legged stride, with Lily on his heels. When they got inside the house, Lily caught sight of Mom's and Dad's backs as they ran through the dining room for the back door.

"What's going on?" Art said.

There was no answer as Lily and Art followed them, dodging dining room chairs. If their parents *had* said anything, they would never have heard it. The din in the backyard had risen to a raucous tangle of screams that drowned out everything else.

Art stopped so abruptly in the doorway, Lily ran into him. She wriggled her way in beside him and stared.

There on the grass just beyond the patio was her ten-year-old brother, Joe, entangled with another body whose fists were pounding on Joe's back. It was like WWE right on the lawn, complete with screams that made Lily's blood run cold.

Mom was on them in a flash, snatching the foreign body by the back of the T-shirt and barking, "All right, break it up! That's enough! I said enough!"

She was doing her coach thing, which Joe responded to by letting Dad pull him out of the fray, red-faced, brown eyes spewing sparks.

The other person continued to scream and kick and grope to get out of Mom's grip. Mom hadn't been a high school coach for twenty years for nothing, but this little person was giving her a challenge. Mom got both the arms pinned down, the body flattened against hers. Then she captured one kicking leg with her own, so that the other one had to stop kicking too, if the child was going to stand at all. Mom had no hands left to clap one over the mouth, though, and it was going full tilt, spitting out words Lily had heard only on an R-rated movie she'd seen by mistake at somebody's house.

"Just let me at her, Dad!" Joe was screaming. "I just wanna—"

"That's it—it's over," Dad said. His usually calm professor's voice had that stern edge that didn't come often but snapped obedience out of any Robbins kid when it did.

But Joe didn't exactly snap into obedience. He stopped screaming, but he was breathing like a mad bulldog and straining against Dad's arms.

*Yikes!* Lily thought. Granted, Joe was usually an absurd little creep, but except for wrestling Art for the remote on the living room floor, she'd never seen him hit anybody before. Much less a girl.

As Lily looked at the tiny, wiry person Mom was still trying to get under control, it was hard to tell what gender she was. She had very short dark hair that might be curly if it were allowed to grow more than a half inch long. Art hadn't been exaggerating when he said she'd gotten a haircut. Buzz was more like it.

The girl continued to shout a stream of words that were now starting to sound hoarse. Lily watched her face twist into a scowl of large, rubbery mouth and big front teeth.

*So this is Tessa,* Lily thought. She looked more like seven than nine, tiny and skinny as she was—though that hadn't seemed to bother her when she was pounding Joe.

Lily looked back at her little brother. He was wiping his bloody nose on his sleeve. Lily felt herself shrinking against Art, but he pulled himself out of the doorway and headed for Dad, who was looking a little winded.

"I'll hold him, Dad," Art said.

Joe opened his mouth, obviously to protest, but Art clapped a hand over it and, pinning Joe's arms, lifted him up and held him sideways.

Dad was now standing between the two captives, arms spread in his that's-enough pose. Tessa was winding down to a croak, though she was still struggling against Mom's iron grip.

"That's it," Dad said. "It's over. When you two are ready to sit down here and talk about it, we'll get it sorted out."

Art gave Dad a you've-gotta-be-kidding look. Lily agreed. Besides, her ears were still hurting from the last bunch of stuff that had come out of Tessa's mouth.

Mom sat with Tessa on one of the metal patio chairs, where she plastered her arms back and held her down. Dad nodded to Art, who sat down with Joe. Lily started to slide toward the steps.

"Join us, Lil," Mom said.

Lily didn't even consider arguing with her. She just tried to be invisible as she took the chair farthest away from everybody.

"All right," Dad said, "we're going to talk this out. Joe — you tell me what happened."

Joe opened his mouth, but Tessa beat him to the punch with a scream of, "He tried to —"

"You'll get your turn," Mom said.

Tessa stiffened and glared at Joe. For the first time, Lily got a look at her face untwisted and discovered that Tessa did have one feminine feature. Her eyes were a clear, mossy green and even bigger than Zooey's. They were fringed with dark, curly eyelashes, the likes of which even Ashley Adamson couldn't achieve with her ton of mascara.

"Joe?" Dad said.

"You told me to show her around the backyard," Joe said, boring an eyehole through Tessa's forehead. "That took, like, about seven seconds, so then I asked her if she played soccer or anything." Joe narrowed his brown, doe-like eyes to slits. "She goes, 'Better than you can, I bet.' So I go, 'Okay, I'll go get a ball, and we'll find out.' And then she jumps me! I didn't even do anything—she just wigged out!"

"I did not—you stinkin' liar!"

*She even talks like a boy,* Lily thought. *A tough boy.* She shuddered. *She reminds me of Shad Shifferdecker.*

No, even Shad wasn't that bad anymore—not like this girl who was going to live here forever and be her sister. Lily felt nauseous again.

"You can have a turn, Tessa," Dad was saying to her. "But there will be no name calling. Just tell us what happened, from your side."

Tessa mumbled something between her rubbery lips. Everybody on the patio leaned forward.

"What did you say, hon?" Mom said.

"I said I couldn't let that kid dis me. I had to do what I had to do."

Dad looked puzzled.

"She means disrespect her," Art said.

"Oh," Dad said. "He showed you disrespect?"

"Yeah."

"I did not!"

Dad put up a hand in Joe's direction. "And then you tried to beat him to a pulp."

Tessa nodded. For the first time, she stopped squirming, as if she'd finally been understood.

*I sure don't get it,* Lily thought. Even Shad Shifferdecker on his worst day had never operated under logic like that. *If she'd just waited and seen Joe play, it wouldn't have been that big a deal,* she thought. Joe had, after all, had to sit out the spring soccer season because of an injury. He'd only just started baseball after having to lie around for two months.

Dad inched his chair closer to Tessa. "Being part of this family is going to be a big adjustment for you, Tessa," he said. The stern voice was gone. This was the understanding voice that always made Lily cry. Tessa did not appear to be anywhere close to tears. "I don't want to throw a lot of rules at you right away," Dad went on. "But I do have to tell you this—we don't settle misunderstandings in this family by screaming and fighting."

Mom cleared her throat. She and Dad exchanged a look.

"So let's just work on the hitting for right now," Dad said.

*No! Work on the screaming too!* Lily wanted to say. Her hands were still clammy and shaky from hearing it.

"If you feel like you want to hit somebody," Mom said, "you come hit Dad or me." Her mouth twitched. "We can handle you."

"I can handle her," Art said.

Lily looked at him quickly. He wasn't looking a whole lot less ticked off than Joe.

"Let's make this a parent thing," Dad said. He looked at Tessa. "No hitting the other kids—is that clear?"

Tessa muttered a begrudging yes. Lily would have bet everything she owned—including China and Otto—that she didn't really mean it.

*It's a good thing I'm going to have horseback riding to keep me busy,* Lily thought. *I don't want to be around this little devil child!*

"Lil," Mom said.

25

Lily jumped as if she'd been shot.

"I think it would be good for Tessa to get settled in her own space. Why don't you and I give her a hand?"

Before she could stop it, a horror-stricken look she could feel inside leaped across Lily's face. She tried to mask it with an instant smile, but even as she did, her blue eyes met Tessa's green ones and watched them turn cold as stones.

"Sure," Lily said in a too-high voice.

That was all she could say, because Tessa's look had frozen her. Lily was scared right down to her bones.

Chapter 4

Lily let Mom and Tessa go ahead of her as they went up the back steps. She looked over her shoulder in the hope that Dad would look at her and she could plead with him with her eyes to save her.

But her father was busy examining Joe's nose, which was swelling up like someone was pumping air into his face. Lily took that image with her all the way up the steps to her old room—Tessa's room.

*What if I say the wrong thing,* Lily thought, heart pounding, *and Tessa thinks I'm dissing her and she jumps me? I could end up with worse than a bloody nose*—

When they got to the room, Tessa fell into a sulky silence. She stood in the middle of the room, looking around and scowling. Mom took that opportunity to give Lily a look that clearly said, "Be nice to her. And start doing it now."

*Okay,* Lily thought. *Maybe I should think how I would feel if it were me.*

*I would be grateful. I would be trying to make friends with these people who were letting me live in their house instead of some old foster home.*

Tessa obviously wasn't feeling quite that way, but Lily looked around her old room and tried to see it the way Tessa was seeing it.

It was freshly painted white. All the holes from Lily's various posters and pictures and mementos of past passions had been filled in and painted over. There were fresh, crisp, white curtains on the window. But everything else was bare so that Tessa could choose her own bedspread and pictures and posters.

Images of posters with devil-eyed girls on them shivered through Lily's brain. She smacked them away and forced a smile. Maybe it was time to do less thinking and more talking.

"This is a great room," Lily said—not looking at Tessa but striding around like a real estate agent. "You have a good view and this big ol' closet—and see, there are shelves in here for your collections and stuff."

"Collections of *what*?" Tessa said.

Reluctantly Lily pulled her head out of the closet to look at her. She was sitting on the bed, arms folded, rubber lip turned up on one side.

"Oh, like—whatever you like to collect," Lily said. She could hear her voice going unnaturally high again as it occurred to her that Tessa probably didn't have little soccer figurines or anything like that. So far, Lily hadn't even seen a suitcase.

"Like leaves or rocks," Lily continued lamely. "We get beautiful leaves here in the fall—only right now it's spring, of course, but you could collect, like, flowers—"

Lily's voice trailed off. Tessa was giving her a you-are-so-weird look. It was all Lily could do not to slink back into the closet and close the door. Only Mom's arched eyebrow and the victorious gleam in Tessa's eyes kept her from doing it. That gleam clearly said Tessa thought she was getting the upper hand. Scared as she was, Lily knew better than to let that happen.

"Joe thinks I'm weird too," Lily said. "You'll figure out I'm not — because you're obviously smarter than him. You'll figure out I'm just unique."

"I hate that kid," Tessa said.

"Okay," Mom said, "let's get you unpacked, Tessa. You need any help?"

Tessa shrugged and picked up a lumpy backpack from the foot of the bed. It was gray, although Lily had a hunch it had been purple at one time. Its zipper appeared to be broken, but there wasn't enough stuff in there for anything to fall out without Tessa's turning it upside down. Instead, she took things out one by one and looked around the room to find a place for everything.

She went about it as if Mom and Lily weren't even there, chin lifted in an I-don't-care manner. Lily suddenly felt as if she were invading Tessa's privacy, and she motioned at Mom with her head toward the door. Mom shook hers.

It didn't take more than about ten minutes for Tessa to put her belongings away, and that was long enough for Lily. With each beat-up, seen-better-days item Tessa pulled out, Lily felt another wave of what felt strangely like loneliness. Tessa had one pair of jeans besides the ones she was now wearing with the grass stains going down one leg, four T-shirts, and a single dress. There were no shoes other than the dingy tennis shoes she had on. Lily wondered if she wore those with the dress.

Once Tessa had tossed a few balls of socks into a drawer, she was finished with clothes and pulled a mishmash of small bottles out of the backpack and lined them up on one of the closet shelves. Lily guessed it was shampoo and conditioner and mouthwash—the kind that came from motels.

"I don't got no toothbrush," Tessa said.

"That's okay—we have extras for company," Lily said.

Mom shot Lily a look. "But we bought one especially for you, Tessa, just in case. It's in the bathroom."

"What color?" Tessa said.

"Red."

"I hate red."

"Don't we have a blue one, Mom?" Lily said.

"I hate blue too," Tessa said.

"We'll deal with the toothbrush situation later," Mom said.

Tessa returned to her backpack and pulled out a battered binder held together by silver duct tape with the dog-eared edges of papers sticking out of it. She held it against her chest as she scoped out the room once again. Her eyes lit on the table Mom had put there for her to use as a desk for doing homework. Lily doubted Tessa would be doing much homework unless she was at gunpoint.

Tessa centered the binder precisely on the table and then looked at Lily.

"Touch this," she said between gritted teeth, "and you're dead meat."

Lily believed her. Nervous chatter bubbled up out of her.

"I know about private stuff. I have a journal that has all my secrets in it, and I've had to teach Joe and Art not to even look at the front *cover*—so you don't have to worry. I have them trained."

Tessa appeared to be ignoring Lily as she opened the binder just far enough to pull something out of it. Then she marched to the wall where her bed was and held the item, a small square photograph with bent corners, up to it, just above the pillows.

"You got a tack or somethin'?" she said.

"How about some tape?" Mom said. "A tack will put a hole in your picture."

"Okay—tape," Tessa said. "I need it right now."

Lily scrambled up. "I'll go get it!" she said. But Mom shook her head and opened a bottom drawer of the dresser. It was filled with markers, glue sticks, paper, pencils, and a roll of tape.

"What's all that stuff?" Tessa said.

"It's your art supplies," Mom said. "We each have our own. Keeps the arguments to a minimum."

Lily waited for Tessa to say, "I hate art." But she just gave the drawer a long look and then snatched the tape out of Mom's hand. Lily had wondered earlier what social skills Art was talking about that Tessa supposedly didn't have. Now she knew.

She watched as Tessa taped the photograph to the wall and then stood back to admire it. It was so small that Lily couldn't tell what it was a picture of from across the room. She sure wasn't going to venture any closer.

To Lily, the photo looked forlorn on that bare white wall all by itself, but Tessa seemed to be satisfied with it as she knelt on the bed studying it as if to be sure nothing on it had changed since she'd put it in her backpack.

Then she turned around to Mom and Lily and said, "I'm done."

"Good," Mom said. "Now you can be thinking about what you want to fill up all this space. Do you have a favorite color for a bedspread?"

It didn't surprise Lily that Tessa said, "Black."

*That stuff in her backpack,* Lily thought. *That was her whole life in there.*

Lily felt that wave of loneliness again—the loneliness she was pretty sure Tessa must feel, down in there someplace. The wave brought with it an idea, and Lily grabbed onto it before it got swept away into her fear of the kid.

"Hey, Tessa," she said. "Do you like stuffed animals?"

Tessa studied her face for a moment and then shrugged. "I guess," she said.

"If you do, I have, like, a hundred of them up in my room. Well, maybe not a hundred, but a lot. You could come up and see if there's one you would want for your bed."

"I guess," Tessa said. "I did have a bear at the last place I was livin', but the cat peed on it, and the lady threw it away."

"Gross me out and make me icky," Lily said. "Didn't she believe in washing machines?"

Tessa shrugged and followed Mom out of the room. Lily sighed deeply.

*We just had a conversation,* she told herself. *Maybe this isn't gonna be so bad.* She stepped lightly on the stairs up to the attic room, smiling a private smile. *I'm so glad I'm doing this,* she thought. *This is a God-thing.*

Mom pushed Lily's door open, and the three of them went in. Tessa stopped just inside the doorway, and Lily watched her stiffen. Lily looked nervously at Mom, who put her finger to her lips and watched Tessa as she moved slowly about the room. She scrutinized Lily's poster of Shakespeare and the certificate that said Lily was president of the seventh grade at Cedar Hills Middle School and the big photograph of the Girlz in Zooey's basement where they always had Girlz Only meetings. Tessa's eyes glinted as she looked at Lily's art supplies arranged in painted jars on her desk and her bottles of colored water on a tray on her dresser. It was as if she were somehow angry.

Smiling her biggest smile, Lily gave the bed a flourish with her hand and said, "So here's the stuffed animals."

She was about to suggest some that Tessa might be interested in adopting when Tessa suddenly flung herself at the bed. She crawled off of it holding China by the neck. He was almost as tall as she was and certainly wider.

"I want this one," she said.

Lily could feel her heart sinking down to her belly button. Her room—her *life*—without China—there was no way! Even fear couldn't make her let that happen.

"Um, that's China," she started to say.

And then she heard a low mumble—from under the bed.

Tessa backed away, her eyes narrowed suspiciously. "What's that?" she said.

Lily didn't have to answer. Otto crawled out on his belly like a soldier in an old war movie. When he caught a glimpse of Tessa, he stopped. The mumbling grew to a growl, and Otto bared his teeth.

"Lily," Mom said in a warning tone.

"No, Otto," Lily said. "Tessa's okay—she's staying here now."

Otto wasn't buying it. He crept further out, still growling.

"No, Otto," Lily said.

She went toward him, but she was knocked sideways by China, whom Tessa was swinging around to the front of her so she could hold him like a shield. Her eyes were glittering.

"Don't even think about coming after me, dog," Tessa said. "Or so help me, I'll crush your little skull."

**N**o!"
This time, Lily was the one screaming as she snatched up Otto and held him under her arm, away from Tessa. He barked and snarled and spit, feet pawing the air, just the way Tessa had been doing on the patio.

"Keep him away from me!" Tessa screamed. "I will kill him!"

"No, you will *not*!" Lily screamed back.

With Otto snapping out barks too, the noise level rose so high that Mom had to shout to be heard over it.

"Enough!" she said. "All three of you!"

Only Lily took heed. Tessa lowered her screams to a yell. Otto barked even louder and wriggled in Lily's arms.

"Do something with him, Lil," Mom said.

Lily nodded and made for the closet, where she deposited Otto with a promise that it would only be for a minute and then closed the door. With that, Tessa stopped yelling, but she was still holding China up like a shield. Lily had visions of Otto getting away and taking a bite right out of her panda's mushy middle.

Only now, he was Tessa's panda. She had a stranglehold on his neck that Lily couldn't have gotten loose if she'd wanted to. And she did want to, but Mom was there, obviously watching Lily for signs of going back on her offer.

"I hate that dog," Tessa said.

*You hate everything!* Lily wanted to say. But instead she shook her head. "He's mostly all bark," she said—although that wasn't entirely true. "He'll get used to you—probably." That wasn't exactly honest either, but Lily felt like she had to do something to get that killer gleam out of Tessa's eyes.

"I'm goin' back to my place now," Tessa said.

She turned on her heel, tennis-shoe rubber squeaking on Lily's hardwood floor. When the boys did that, Mom always said, "This is not a basketball court, gentlemen." But to Tessa she said nothing except, "I think that's a great idea."

Tessa left, holding China by the throat again. Lily bit back a list of instructions on how to take care of him and started to follow.

Mom put a hand on the back of Lily's neck and gave it an affectionate squeeze. "Why don't you get some alone time, Lil?" she said. "I'll take over from here."

Lily was so relieved she could have cried. "Just don't let her beat up on China, okay?" she whispered.

Lily wasn't sure, but she thought that as her mother went out the door, she muttered, "Better him than the three of you."

As soon as she heard Tessa's door close downstairs, Lily rescued Otto from the closet, went down to the second-floor hallway, and grabbed the portable phone.

*I have to talk to Reni,* she told herself. *She never screams.*

35

She went down to the first floor and directly into the laundry room, where she curled up on top of the dryer. The second Reni answered the phone, Lily launched forth.

She started with Joe's bloody nose and ended with Tessa's threat to kill Otto. "I've wanted to kill him a couple times myself," Reni said.

"But she really means it!" Lily said.

"No, she does not."

"Uh-HUH! You haven't seen the way her eyes get. She's meaner than anybody I ever met."

"Nuh-uh."

"Yuh-huh."

There was a soft silence, and Lily was glad Reni was being sympathetic. There was no way she was getting through this without her support. It came immediately.

"Well, look," Reni said. "You know you can come over and stay with me any time you want to."

"I might need to," Lily said. "There's no way I'm hanging out with her all the time. She's like a demon seed or something."

"Are you talkin' about me?"

Lily jerked, almost dropping the phone. The laundry room door was open, and Tessa was standing there, green eyes cold. There was no doubt. She had heard the last thing Lily had said, if not more.

*How did she get the door open without me hearing her?* Lily thought. The image of Tessa being able to sneak up on her made Lily absolutely shiver.

"What's going on?" Reni said into the phone.

"I gotta go," Lily said. "I'll call you later."

"What are you gonna tell her *then*?" Tessa said as Lily pushed the off button and scrambled down from the dryer. Tessa widened her eyes. "That I'm possessed?"

That possibility *had* occurred to Lily, but she shook her head—hard.

"I was just joking around with Reni," she said. "She's my best friend—we do that."

"Yeah. Right."

"We do!" Lily didn't like the way her voice was sliding up, and she forced it down. "What did you come in here for anyway?"

"Because I live here, Mutant."

"Mutant?" Lily said. "What's that?"

For the first time that day, Lily saw Tessa smile. It wasn't pretty, because it never reached her eyes. They stayed cold and hard.

"Look it up, since you're so smart," Tessa said. Then she did that rubber-squealing thing with her shoe again and left.

Lily clicked the door shut and slid down to the floor onto a pile of dirty clothes. Her mouth felt like she'd been sucking on a cotton ball.

*Who is this child?* she thought. *Did Mom and Dad really check her out? Are they sure she doesn't have a prison record or something?*

It wasn't hard to conjure up an image of Tessa pacing around a cell and then going to the bars and banging on them and screaming, "Let me out of here, you bunch of mutants—or I'll crush your skulls!"

At the very worst, Lily had imagined Shad Shifferdecker slouching in a chair in the discipline office, giving the vice principal lip. It had never occurred to her that Shad would threaten death to a dog.

And the worst part of it was that what Tessa had just said was true: "I live here, Mutant."

*What's a mutant?* Lily thought. She was afraid to look it up.

From beyond the laundry room door, Lily could hear her mother calling her to come set the table. The thought of sitting down at the table with that girl made her lose her appetite, even though she knew Mom had planned homemade pizza for Tessa's first supper with them.

The kitchen smelled like garlic and melted cheese, a combination that normally made Lily's stomach growl and brought Art and Joe running from miles away. But no one was hanging around as Lily set the dining room table with a red-and-white checkered tablecloth and candles stuck in old bottles with wax dripping down. Those usually came out only when they had company. In fact, Lily realized, they ate in the dining room only when there were guests.

*But Tessa's not a guest,* she thought. *She lives here now.*

Lily plunked a fork down next to her plate and shook her head. What was the point? She couldn't eat now if somebody stuffed it down her throat.

When the pizzas were pulled out of the oven, everybody came to the table at a crawl. Dad and Tessa emerged from Dad's study together, which sent a jealous pang through Lily. That was where *she* talked to Dad. Couldn't they find another place?

Nobody said much at the table at first—except for Dad, who prayed. Lily sneaked a peek at Tessa. She was sitting back in her chair while everybody else had their heads bowed, and she was checking out the china cabinet with her eyes.

*Mom better put a lock on that,* Lily thought.

"Okay," Mom said. "Who wants pepperoni?"

"I hate pepperoni," Tessa said.

Lily rolled her eyes. *Big surprise.*

"I'll take a couple of slices of that," Dad said. He sounded to Lily way more enthusiastic than he ever got over pizza. Dad usually got so involved in his thoughts or in the conversation, Mom could have served him rubber bands and he probably wouldn't have noticed.

"How about plain cheese, then?" Mom said to Tessa.

"What else you got?" Tessa said.

"This isn't Domino's," Joe said.

Mom shot him a look.

"We got cheese, we got pepperoni, we got sausage and green peppers," Art said. "And that's more choices than we usually get, so go for it."

"You don't got any anchovies?" Tessa said.

"Sick," Joe said.

"What are anchovies?" Lily said.

Art gave a half grin. "Little fishies—aaand they stink."

"Do not," Tessa said.

"If Art says they stink, they stink," Joe said.

"No anchovies, stinky or unstinky," Mom said firmly. "What'll it be, Tessa?"

"Pepperoni, I guess."

There was a sense of relief as a piece of pizza was finally delivered to Tessa's plate, but that was short lived. She took a bite out of it and promptly made a face and spit it out onto her plate.

"Sick!" Joe said again.

"What's the matter?" Dad said, peering at her over his glasses.

"That stuff tastes like dog poop!"

Lily clapped her hand over her mouth. Art snickered.

"You've tasted dog poop before, then," he said.

"We're not going there, Art," Mom said.

"She brought it up," Art said. "I was just clarifying."

"You were just being a smart—" Tessa started to say, but Dad interrupted her with "Remember what we just talked about."

"What did you talk about?" Joe said.

"None of your business," Mom said.

"Yeah—just butt out of my business, loser!" Tessa said to him.

"Who you callin' a loser?"

It went downhill from there. When Lily asked if she could be excused, Dad nodded vaguely in her direction. She was sure nobody missed her as she scurried up to her room and curled up in the corner of her bed. Otto climbed up to join her. It was lonesome without China. She was lonesome, period. Her whole family was downstairs, and yet so much had changed in one afternoon. It didn't even seem like her family anymore.

She slid her hand between her mattresses and pulled out her talking-to-God journal.

"We gotta talk, God," she said out loud. " I don't know if I can handle this—"

Lily wrote furiously until her hand ached. She had to put down her gel pen and shake out her fingers. But the rest of her felt better. After all, hadn't God always been there? Had God ever given up on any situation she was in? And hadn't she been in plenty of them?

"I know you'll either send her back where she belongs or shape her up so we can stand her," Lily wrote on the last line. "'Cause that's the way you are. You don't give up 'til I figure out what I'm supposed to do."

She started to close the journal, and then she had another thought.

"I think you have given me horses right now to help me get through this," she wrote. "I'm going to have something else to concentrate on beside us having Tessa here."

Then she put her journal back under the mattress and hugged Otto. "It's gonna happen with the horses," she told him. "After all—I'm a natural."

# Chapter 6

As the next week unfolded, however, it turned out to be difficult for Lily to keep her focus on horses.

In the first place, she couldn't possibly think about anything but Tessa when Tessa was around, because Tessa—as far as Lily was concerned—plunked herself in the center of everything and then proceeded to turn it upside down.

Sunday morning she refused to get out of bed for church until Mom and Dad both went into her room and spent half an hour coaxing her. Joe asked Lily how come Tessa got all that when all he ever got was, "I'm counting, Joe."

When Tessa finally did get it together to go out the door, she was wearing her second pair of jeans, very baggy with a slice out of each knee, and a T-shirt that said "Bite Me." Mom let her keep the jeans, but there was a screaming battle over the shirt—Tessa screaming and Mom silently taking the shirt off of her and replacing it with one that had "Angel" written on it in glitter.

"Who's she trying to kid?" Art mumbled under his breath.

Lily was glad Tessa would be in Joe's Sunday school class and not hers. Joe didn't put that together until they were at the door. Lily didn't hang around to see how it turned out.

All during church, Tessa sat with her arms folded across her chest, glaring at the pastor as if he alone were responsible for all her misery, past and present, and making remarks out of the side of her mouth. "He's so full of himself." "Yeah, right, preacher—and I'm the Easter bunny."

The one that screamed in Lily's head was the one Tessa said several times: "Like there's really a God. Right."

"Dad?" Lily whispered to her father on the way to the car after the service. "Did you know Tessa doesn't believe in God?"

"I think that's pretty obvious, Lilliputian," Dad said. "But give her time with us. She'll come around."

*Do you have about ninety years?* Lily wanted to say. She had to remind herself that God didn't give up. If she'd been God, she would have given up on the kid a long time ago.

Lily was glad to see the next day come, when she could go to school and not have to see Tessa for at least six hours. She got dressed in record time, hoping she could get a ride with Dad instead of going in the van with Mom, Joe, and, of course, Tessa. But Mom told her they were going to try to do things just as they always did so Tessa would get used to the routine. It looked to Lily like Tessa was creating her own routine.

Once again she had to be hauled out of bed, and once again, Mom put the kibosh on the "Bite Me" shirt, with the promise that they would go shopping that evening and get her some appropriate clothes.

"And was she grateful?" Lily asked the Girlz at the bench that morning when she got to school. "No, she was not! She went into this screaming fit about how Mom was always putting her down!"

42

"Your mom never put anybody down in her life," Reni said.

"Your mom is nice lady," Kresha put in. She gave Lily a sympathetic pat on the shoulder.

"You bet she's nice," Lily said. "She didn't do a thing when Tessa said she wasn't going to school *or* when she tried to kick Mom when she picked her up to carry her to the car."

"She picked her up?" Zooey said, eyes popping. "And she's nine?"

"She's way little," Lily said. "Smaller than Suzy even."

They all gazed at Suzy as if to get a visual on Tessa's miniature stature.

"Did she finally shut up?" Reni said.

Lily nodded. "Yeah, but only because she, like, wore herself out. Mom dropped me off first because she had to take her in the first day."

Suzy shook her head. "I'm glad she doesn't go here," she said.

Zooey was counting on her fingers. "By the time she starts here, we'll be sophomores at the high school," she said.

"Dat is goot," Kresha put in.

"If she's still here."

They all looked at Lily.

"What do you mean, if she's still here?" Reni said. "She lives with you now. Your parents are adopting her. They can't just give her back."

"They can't?" Zooey said.

Lily shook her head miserably. "No," she said. "They can't."

It was too depressing to think about. For the rest of the day, Lily drew pictures of horses in her notebooks when she finished her work and imagined the adoption people coming and taking Tessa away, saying they'd made a terrible mistake and given them the wrong kid. She couldn't wait to be with all the Girlz at their meeting at Zooey's after school. She was building up uglies, and she needed to be with her friends, where there were no uglies.

But at the end of their last class, just after Lily finished making sure that everybody was going to be at Girlz Only, she looked up to see Mom motioning to her from the classroom doorway. Lily stopped breathing until she got to her.

"What's wrong?" she said. "Why aren't you at work? Did something happen?"

"I had to take a personal leave day," Mom said. She took Lily by the sleeve and led her out into the hallway crowd. Working in a high school herself, she wasn't bothered by the throng of kids surging toward the lockers.

"Do you need anything from your locker?" she said.

Lily shook her head. "But I don't get it—what are you doing here?"

"I'm taking you home, and then I need to get word to Art—"

"What's going *on*?"

Mom continued to maneuver Lily toward the stairs. "Tessa left school today."

"What do you mean she left?"

"She just slipped out of the classroom when the teacher wasn't looking—"

"Wasn't looking? Didn't you tell the teacher never to take her eyes off of that kid?"

Mom looked at Lily as they started down the steps. "Do you want to know what's going on or not?"

"Sorry," Lily said.

"She was walking home when the truant officer found her and picked her up. Apparently he earned his salary today—she gave him quite a run for his money. They kept her at Juvenile Hall until they could get in touch with me. I picked her up and took her back to school and stayed with her all day. But I have to get back for practice—"

They were at the van by now, and Lily couldn't stand it any longer. "So where is she now? You didn't leave her alone at the house, did you? She'll kill Otto!"

Mom shook her ponytail and motioned for Lily to get in the car.

"Half of what she says is just talk, Lil," she said.

"What about the other half?" Lily said.

"We'll take the other half one thing at a time." Mom slid into the driver's seat and leaned her head back, eyes closed. It wasn't something Lily had seen her mother do often. She could usually take anything on without so much as catching her breath.

"Are you okay, Mom?" Lily said.

Mom lifted her head and started up the van with a brisk twist of her wrist. "Just regrouping. I'm taking you home so you can do homework with Joe and Tessa. That will keep everybody focused and busy. Art will be in charge until Dad gets home, and he should be there within the hour."

"But Girlz Only will be over by then!" Lily said. "Reni has violin lessons and Suzy has soccer, so we can only be there an hour!"

"I'm sorry, Lil," Mom said. "It can't be helped this time. Just hang in there with me, okay?"

"But why do I have to be there? I do my homework in my room."

"Because you have a calming influence on Tessa. Without you there, it's her and the boys. She seems to get more violent with males."

"She hates me," Lily said. She folded her arms across her chest.

"She thinks she hates everything and everybody." Mom's mouth twitched. "Or didn't you notice?"

Lily didn't think that was funny. She didn't talk all the way home. Or, for that matter, any other day that week when Art picked her up after school and they both went home to do homework with Tessa and Joe. If you asked Lily, it was more like refereeing.

Joe tried—at first—to just do his assignments, but Tessa made so many comments about his being a loser, he let loose the first day by throwing a pencil at her. She took that as an open invitation to crawl across the table, grab his almost-completed math paper, and rip it to shreds—all before Art could even get up out of his chair.

The second day—when it still "couldn't be helped"—Lily decided to try to get Tessa working on her own stuff so she wouldn't heckle Joe, who finished his assignments at light speed and disappeared.

"What's your language arts assignment?" Lily said.

"How should I know?" Tessa said.

"Didn't you write it down on your assignment sheet?"

"Don't got no assignment sheet."

"Sure you do," Lily said.

She reached for Tessa's brand-new backpack—black, of course. Tessa sprang from the chair and grabbed Lily's wrist. Lily let out a scream, which brought Art out of the kitchen where he was heating up Hot Pockets in the microwave.

"What's going on?" he said.

Tessa flung Lily's wrist from her hand and said, "Tell her not to touch my stuff, or I'll rip her fingers off!"

"I was just gonna see if she had an assignment sheet!" Lily said.

"O-kaaay," Art said to Tessa. "She won't touch anything of yours, all right. But you're not gonna rip her fingers off. That's not cool."

*Ya think?* Lily put both hands behind her back and curled her fingers into protective balls.

"Is there an assignment sheet in there?" Art said, nodding at the backpack that Tessa was now clutching to her chest.

"Is it that thing where Mrs. Lame writes down what she thinks I'm gonna do for homework?"

"Mrs. Lame?" Lily said. "Is your teacher's name actually Mrs. Lame?"

"No, Mutant," Tessa said, lip cocked. "It's just what I call her. You're Mutant, and she's Mrs. Lame. And that kid I hate is Loser."

Art folded his arms lazily. "So — Tess — do I get a nickname?"

"It's Tess-a," she said, glaring at him.

"Oh, so let me get this straight," Art said. "You can call us anything you want, but we can't call you what we want to call you. I don't get the difference."

Tessa didn't even have to think about her answer. "The difference is that I can pound any one of you for calling me a name. You guys won't pound me."

"Joe would — in a second!" Lily said.

"No, he wouldn't, because he's a loser. He does what they tell him to."

" 'They' being Mom and Dad," Art said. He looked to Lily as if he were fascinated by this conversation. Lily was ready to climb the dining room wall. She pointed to the backpack.

"So why don't you take out that sheet the teacher wrote out for you?" Lily said.

Tessa dragged out a wadded-up piece of paper with the straight, perfect handwriting of a fourth-grade teacher on the lines and several random drawings of what looked like creatures from outer space on the borders.

"You draw those?" Art said, looking over her shoulder.

Tessa snatched the paper from his view and gave him her cold, hard look.

Lily finally managed to get a look at the paper and saw that Tessa was supposed to use each one of the spelling words in a sentence. Lily had always kind of liked that exercise. Tessa hated it.

"This is stupid," she said. "Who cares about this anyway?"

"Just try the first one," Lily said. "What's the word?"

Tessa looked at it and shrugged.

"Woman," Lily read. "Oh, that oughta be easy. Think of a sentence with the word 'woman' in it."

Tessa gave her a joyless smile. "That woman that teaches our class is lame."

"I don't think you can write that," Lily said. "How about, 'That woman who teaches our class is nice.'"

Tessa snorted. Lily handed her a pencil and pushed a piece of paper toward her.

"Write it, and you get a Hot Pocket," Art said from the kitchen.

"I hate Hot Pockets," Tessa muttered.

She picked up the pencil, and with a sigh that seemed to come from her knees pressed it so hard against the paper that Lily was sure the point was going to break. She carved a large, lopsided T into the paper and then put the pencil down.

"What's wrong?" Lily said.

"My hand hurts. I hate writing."

"Okay—you rested—finish the word," Lily said. At this rate, the Hot Pockets were going to need reheating.

Sighing again, Tessa took up the pencil, clenching it like Lily had seen Joe do when he was in first grade, and engraved A H T into the paper. The pencil then went down again.

"T A H T?" Lily said. "What's that spell?"

"THAT," Tessa said. "What else would it spell?"

"You don't know how to spell 'that'?" Lily said

"Whoa, Lil." Art said. He put the plate of Hot Pockets next to Tessa and gave her a nudge. "Most brilliant people can't spell. That's why God invented spell-check. Have a Hot Pocket."

Lily was immediately sorry. She even started to say so to Tessa. But before she could open her mouth, Tessa gave her the coldest, hardest look yet. And then a glint took shape in her eyes. For the first time in her life, Lily saw what true mean looked like.

"Maybe it would be better if Dad helped you with your homework," Lily said quickly.

"You mean Nerd?" Tessa said.

Lily felt her face go blotchy.

"Why don't you do your homework upstairs, Lil?" Art said. "I got it from here."

Lily was glad to go. She had a paper for English to copy over for Mrs. Reinhold's hawklike inspection, and she sure hadn't had a chance to work on it while she was prodding Tessa to get *her* homework done.

But she didn't do it right away when she got to her room. She lay on her bed, staring at the ceiling, planning what she was going to do to keep from plucking Tessa's nose hairs out—one by one.

After writing ten pages in her talking-to-God journal that night, Lily did have a plan—a don't-give-up plan. She was going to have to talk to Mom and Dad about her horse right away. She had to get the ball rolling.

The next morning, she was able to squeeze out two minutes alone with Mom before the screaming began, and asked her if they could talk tonight.

"Just you, me, and Dad?" she said. "It'll only take ten minutes, I promise."

"You feeling a little neglected, Lil?" Mom said.

"How'd you know?"

"Because I'd feel that way if I were you. Tessa is taking all of our attention right now. But I think she's starting to come around."

Lily grunted.

"How about after Tessa goes to bed?" Mom said. "Then we know we won't be interrupted."

Lily grinned and threw her arms around her mother's neck. "I love you, Mom," she said. "You're the best."

"Right back at ya, Lil," Mom said, and gave her a squeeze.

For the first time since Tessa had arrived, Lily felt like something might be okay after all.

*I'm not even going to complain about Tessa at the bench today,* she told herself when she got to school. *It's not all about her anymore.*

When she reached the bench, the Girlz were all there. Zooey was surveying Kresha.

"Kresh," Zooey said. "Are you planning to brush your hair today, honey?"

Kresha put her hand up to her tousled head. "I did not do it?"

"Doesn't look like it," Reni said.

Kresha deflated. "I do not ewen have brush wit me," she said.

"I have one in my bag," Lily said. "I'll probably have to dig for it—"

She unzipped her backpack and moved her English homework aside to get to the brush. She froze, holding her breath.

"What's wrong?" Zooey said. "There's something wrong, I can see it on your face."

Lily *felt* it on her face too. She felt it draining of color as she pulled out the paper she'd copied over with such care last night. Across her words was a single one written in red marker—with black accents.

MOOTENT, it said.

"Moo-tent?" Reni said. "I don't get it—"

"No, mutant," Zooey said. "I've heard them say it on *Star Trek.* It's like some kind of freak or something."

"Why did you write that, Lily?" Suzy said. She was darting her eyes around nervously, as if she were convinced it was something that was going to get them all in trouble somehow.

"I didn't." Lily said. "*She* did—all over my English homework!"

"Tessa?" Reni said.

"How come she wrote 'mutant'?" Zooey said.

"Who cares! It's my homework! I can't turn it in to Mrs. Reinhold this way—and it's due first period!"

The vow not to vent to the girls about Tessa snapped in two, and Lily exploded. She described the devil child all over again, topping it off with this latest travesty.

"What are you going to do?" Suzy said.

"I'm gonna have to copy the whole thing over," Lily said. She stuffed the paper back into her pack and made for the stairs. "I am *so* mad!" she said. "And Mom and Dad better do something about this!"

By the time the tardy bell rang, Lily had her paper copied over. It wasn't as neat and perfect as the original—but it didn't have something evil scrawled across it either. One thing was for sure—this meeting with Mom and Dad had to go well tonight.

The vocabulary exercise Mrs. Reinhold gave them was easy, and Lily raced through it. When she turned it in, she asked Mrs. R. for a hall pass to the library.

For the rest of the period, Lily scoured the library for everything she could find about horses and checked out all the related books they would let her. All day she hauled them around with her, and every chance she got she studied and made notes from them. It seemed like it was a God-thing that Mr. Chester was absent and the sub gave them a study hall. Lily went to a corner and put together her full presentation, complete with drawings of several breeds she thought would be good. The only thing she needed was Herbie's phone number, which she asked Suzy for at the lockers after school.

"I don't know it by heart," Suzy said. "Why do you want it?"

"I'm going to take lessons," Lily said. "He told me I was a natural."

Reni's eyes narrowed. "Wait a minute," she said. "Are you starting up another one of your things?"

"No, Lily," Zooey said. "I didn't even like riding that much — no offense, Suzy."

"I didn't say it was a Girlz Only thing," Lily said. "It's something I want to do."

"Doesn't work that way," Reni said matter-of-factly. "Whatever you get into, we always end up getting into it with you."

"Why we not?" Kresha said, smiling big. "We are the Girlz!"

"And I don't want to ride horses anymore." Zooey's voice was going up into a whine, which was irritating Lily.

"I don't have time to talk about it right now," Lily said.

"You have Tessa duty again?" Reni said.

Suzy shuddered. "Don't take it personally, Lily — but I don't think I ever even want to meet your new sister."

"She is *so* not my sister!" Lily said. And then before she could explode again, she headed for the front entrance.

The homework session, supper, and getting Tessa to go to bed all seemed to drag that night. Lily tried to hurry things up by setting up her presentation in Dad's study while her parents were upstairs calmly quieting Tessa's screams. They had gotten pretty good at getting her to hush up, but they'd made no progress in stopping the wall banging that went on until Tessa exhausted herself and dropped off to sleep in mid-bang.

When that finally happened, Lily was ready. She had her drawings arranged on an easel and two copies of her proposal, neatly printed out on the computer, to put into their hands.

"What's all this, Lilliputian?" Dad said.

"If you guys'll sit down, I'll explain everything," Lily said.

They both looked a little amused, but they took the seats Lily had set for them and watched and listened as Lily went through her well-rehearsed presentation. She hadn't been quite sure of the ending until now, but the whole thing went so well that her last line fell like silk from her lips.

"So," she said, "I think you can see that the best possible thing for all of us would be for me to get a horse for my birthday."

There was a stunned silence. Mom's and Dad's faces were sober, their eyes blinking. Lily could feel her heart start to race. This was it. They were so impressed — they were going to say yes.

But they didn't. Instead, Dad said, "Come here, Lilliputian," and patted the chair next to him. Woodenly, Lily perched there.

"So can I have my horse?" she said.

"No, hon," Mom said. "No, you can't — "

"But why?"

Between the two of them, Mom and Dad rattled off a list of reasons, none of which made sense to Lily.

They had no place to keep a horse.

Having a horse was a huge responsibility, one they couldn't help her with right now.

What would happen to the horse when the Robbinses all went to England in August for a whole year?

Lily argued with every one of those reasons — except the last one Dad gave her. "We simply don't have money for an investment like that right now," he said.

"But what about your promotion and your book that's selling all those copies?"

"We discussed this before we even started the adoption proceedings," Mom said. "That money is going into sharing our blessings with another human being and hopefully changing her life."

"You mean Tessa," Lily said. She could feel her lip curling at the corner, the way Tessa's did. "So you had to buy her new clothes and stuff. That can't cost that much."

"Lily," Dad said. He had dropped the "putian" and was looking at her with serious eyes. "It costs money to adopt a child. And now that we are responsible for Tessa, we have to pay for her therapy, get her involved in activities the way you three kids are, start a college fund for her—"

Lily had a dozen answers for all of those. But it was clearly pointless. Mom and Dad were watching her, waiting for her to finish getting it all out of her system before they said their final no. She'd seen that look before. It did no good to argue with it.

"Now," Dad said as Lily started to get up. "We *can* compromise with you, though. We can pay for some riding lessons."

"With Herbie?" Lily said.

"Sure. You seemed to like him."

"I told you—he said I was a natural."

"Then Herbie it is."

Mom and Dad seemed relieved that the conversation was over. Mom didn't even warn Lily not to go overboard with "this horse thing." They both looked like they were too tired to discuss it anymore.

*So Tessa is getting all the attention—all the breaks—and now all the money too! We're their real kids. Tessa's the devil's child!*

Upstairs, Lily picked up the phone to call Suzy and get Herbie's number before her parents decided they'd better get braces or something for Tessa instead. Before she could start dialing, it rang.

"Hello?" Lily said.

"Hey—Robbins," said a raspy voice. "This is Shifferdecker."

Shad?" Lily said.

Then she rolled her eyes. Of course it was Shad. How many people did she know named Shifferdecker?

The real question should have been *Why are you calling me?*

"So—what's up?" Lily said.

"Nothin'," Shad said.

There was dead silence.

Lily sighed impatiently. "Then why did you call me, Shad?"

She could almost see him shrugging before he answered. "Just wanted to see what was goin' on."

"Oh," Lily said.

"I gotta go."

And then he hung up.

*What was that about?* she thought as she went on up to her room, leaving the phone behind. She couldn't call Suzy now—it was 9:02. None of the Girlz' parents let them make phone calls after 9:00, and Suzy's dad was really strict about it.

"I'll take care of it tomorrow, first thing," she told Otto as he joined her on the bed, ready for her talking-to-God session. "And don't worry—I'm not gonna love any horse more than I do you." She snuggled closer to him and sighed. "I miss China."

Before she could get into a vision of Tessa using her panda to slam against the wall, Lily wrote—all about working as hard as she had to to get her lessons set up.

It seemed to pay off. By the next afternoon, right after school, she had her first lesson scheduled for Saturday morning and had talked Art into taking her—well, bribed him was more like it, promising to do his chores all week long.

After that, three days seemed like an eternity to wait. It was all Lily could talk about with the Girlz, though at least it was better than always venting about Tessa.

"I want to be the best horsewoman I can," she told them at lunch the third day.

"Horsewoman," Zooey said. "Wow."

"Here it comes," Reni said. "I told you, guys. Can't you see it in her eyes?"

"I'm not asking anybody to get on a horse," Lily said. "I'm just doing it because—well, I'm just doing it."

"I'd go with you," Reni said. She ripped open a bag of Sun Chips and looked directly at Lily. "At least then we'd get to see you."

"You know it's not my fault I can't do stuff after school right how," Lily said. "I hate it."

"I think I hate Tessa already, and I haven't even seen her," Zooey said.

"Yeah, well, she probably hates you too," Lily said. "She hates everything."

That night Reni called, fortunately after the nightly foot banging had stopped. "You know what you need?" she said.

"What?"

"You need some Girlz time."

"How am I supposed to get that? It's all about Tessa now — I don't get time to do anything."

"What about tomorrow? What about your riding lesson?"

"Yeah —" Lily said. "But you guys aren't —"

"What if I came?" Reni said.

Lily could feel her face lighting up. "Really?"

"I kinda already asked my parents. My mom said she thought it would be good for me to do something besides play the violin." She gave a grunt. "My dad says I could break my arm and not be able to play for six weeks and then I'd fall behind on everything —"

"So — you're coming?" Lily said.

"You want me to?"

"Yes! We'll even pick you up — I know Art will — and Reni, I got the cutest bandana — it's bright yellow."

They talked, nonstop, until Reni's dad made her hang up. It was, after all, 9:01.

The next morning, Lily was outfitted — her best jeans, a flannel shirt she talked Art out of, and the yellow bandana tied around her neck. Life was good, until she got to the kitchen.

Tessa was already there, complaining that her Rice Krispies were soggy.

"You're the one left them sitting in the milk for ten minutes," Joe told her.

She picked up the bowl, but Mom intercepted it before she could throw its contents into Joe's face.

"Can I take mine in the family room and watch TV?" Joe said.

Lily decided to skip cereal and got a Nutri-Grain bar out of the pantry.

"Where's Art?" she said. "We have to leave—we have to pick up Reni."

"How about if I be your chauffeur this morning?"

It was Dad, standing in the kitchen doorway. He had on his I'm-not-a-professor-today look, bright-eyed and focused on Lily.

"Yes!" Lily said.

It was only a few streets over to Reni's house, and Dad seemed to want to take full advantage of that. He started in the minute they pulled out of the driveway.

"This is all very hard, Lilliputian, I know it is. And it's going to be even harder for those two weeks I'll be in England setting things up for us—finding us a place to live while we're there—that sort of thing."

"You're lucky. You'll be away from *her*." Lily immediately bit at her lip.

"I hear you," Dad said. "I sometimes think, boy, this is so tough on Joe and Lily and Art—maybe we made a mistake." He shook his head. "But this has been—what do you always call it?—a God-thing. I know that. So—I'm getting through it by completely trusting God."

"Okay," Lily said. And then she sighed.

When Lily and Reni ran into the stables, Herbie met them with a grin. It was the first time Lily noticed that he had a space between his two front teeth. She decided she liked that.

"How are you girlies doing?" he said.

"We are *so* ready to ride," Lily said.

"That's what I like to hear." Herbie looked at Reni. "Now, you, Reni-girl, are going to be riding Patches, and Georgie's going to be giving you your lesson. He's a saddle horse, so he rides nice and smooth." He then looked at Lily from under the brim of his huge hat. "And you, Lily-girl, will be riding—"

"Big Jake?" Lily said. "Please say it's Big Jake."

Herbie looked at Reni. "What's going to happen if I don't let her ride Big Jake?"

"She'll freak," Reni said.

He looked, stone-faced, at Lily. "You'll be riding Big Jake—"

"Yes!"

"And I'll be giving you your lesson."

"Yes!"

"But won't we get to ride together?" Reni said.

"We'll let you two ride in the Round Pen after your lessons so you can practice. Later on, we'll let you have free ride, when you're ready."

"How long will that take?" Lily said. "I'm only signed up for five lessons."

"You can always take more. And don't worry about it, Lily-girl. I have a feeling you're going to be trotting on your own before the week's out."

That was all Lily needed to hear. She was at Big Jake's side in a flash, petting his nose and telling him he was wonderful. All the books said to do that.

But learning how to ride Big Jake—*really* ride him—was tons better than reading about it in a book. *Tons* better.

Herbie taught her to get to know Big Jake before she tried to ride him. He explained that birthday-party rides were different because someone else was controlling everything.

Herbie's bright eyes twinkled at Lily. "Supposedly, anyway."

He taught her to stay to the left of Big Jake, between his nose and his neck where the horse could see her. If she came up behind him, Herbie said, she might get kicked.

When she was finally allowed to get on, Herbie rode beside her on Jiminy. He showed her how to pick up the reins and gently get Jake walking, then how to guide him to the left and then to the right by the slightest pull on the reins.

It was all very gentle and slow. Still, when Herbie let her walk Jake around by herself in the Round Pen—Reni was still learning how to make Patches go forward—Lily couldn't help but imagine that the light spring breeze was a wild wind blowing through her hair as it streamed behind her. She felt like a medieval maiden off on a mission.

The next four lessons—every day the next week—got better and better. When Lily wasn't riding, she was decorating her room in everything horse—a slightly torn horse poster she picked up at a yard sale, which she put just above her dresser, and as many drawings of horses as she could crank out to cover the rest of her walls. She tried to make each one look like Big Jake.

"I've totally bonded with Jake," Lily told Reni on the way home Wednesday, their second to the last day.

"Who's Jake?" Art said. "You going out with somebody?"

"No, Clueless," Lily said. "That's my horse."

"Oh—so now it's *your* horse."

Lily sank back into her seat. "It's the closest I'm gonna get."

"But you can always get more lessons," Reni said. "I'm not as good at riding as you are, but I'm gonna ask my parents if I can take some more."

"That would be so cool. I wish the other Girlz could too—and not because it's my latest thing."

"It *is* your latest thing," Art said.

"I already asked them," Reni said. "Kresha's mom doesn't have the money, and Suzy's father says she's in enough lessons already, and you know Zooey won't do it." Reni rolled her eyes. "She says it hurt her rear end."

"It's okay that it's just you and me," Lily said. "I couldn't stand another day with Tessa if it weren't for you."

"Then we *have* to keep riding together," Reni said. "We can't give it up."

Lily agreed. She made up her mind to take care of that as soon as she got home.

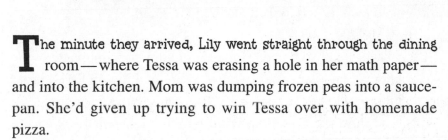

# Chapter 9

The minute they arrived, Lily went straight through the dining room—where Tessa was erasing a hole in her math paper—and into the kitchen. Mom was dumping frozen peas into a saucepan. She'd given up trying to win Tessa over with homemade pizza.

"How was your lesson?" Mom said. "No—I don't even need to ask. I can see it on your face. You've really enjoyed this, haven't you?"

"I have," Lily said. "That's why I want to keep taking lessons. Can I sign up for five more? Tomorrow's my last day—"

She stopped. She could already see the answer in Mom's eyes. They were sympathetic but not encouraging. They had the I'm-sorry-Lily look.

"Why can't I?" Lily said.

"It's all about money, Lil," Mom said. "We did what we could—"

*It's because of her, isn't it?* Lily wanted to scream—louder than Tessa ever had. Maybe Dad was wrong. Maybe God gave up on one person when some *other* person took up all his time.

Clenching her jaw, her fists, her teeth, Lily left the kitchen and rammed through the dining room. Tessa looked up from the hole she had made in the middle of long division.

"What's wrong, Mutant?" she said. "You didn't get what you wanted?"

Lily ignored her and rammed on, but Tessa stopped her at the doorway.

"I know about that," she said. "I used to never get nothin' I wanted."

For a fraction of second, there was no smirk on Tessa's rubbery mouth, no glint of hate or victory in her eyes. She just blinked her curly-edged eyelids and looked like a kid.

"Oh," Lily said.

Then Tessa said, "Too bad, Mutant," and the moment passed.

Until her riding lesson the next day, the only thing on Lily's mind was that this would be the last time she would see Big Jake or Herbie and the last time she'd feel the wind blowing her hair back as she trotted around the Round Pen like a medieval maiden.

"Now that's a long face, that one," Herbie said to her. "What's up, Lily-girl?"

When Lily told him, she started to cry. Herbie's face got long too.

"Big Jake is going to miss you," Herbie said. "I wouldn't be surprised if he went into a deep depression and wouldn't eat without you here every afternoon."

"I'm sorry!" Lily said. She wished he would stop. Her chest was ready to split open as it was.

"I can't have that," Herbie said. He took off his hat and rubbed his bandana-wrapped head. "So what about this? What if you came in, say, every Saturday and helped out around here? You know — help with the horses — although that includes shoveling their poop." He put his hat back on and looked at her, bright-eyed, from under the brim. "That should pay for lessons three days a week. You think?"

"Really?" Lily said. "I could do that—you would do that?"

Herbie nodded. His face was serious. "When I find a rider who shows promise, I like to keep her around. You talk to your parents."

Lily sagged against the stall. Big Jake nuzzled at her cheek.

"You all right, Lily-girl?" Herbie said.

"I am *so* all right," Lily said. "You wouldn't even believe it."

And maybe, she thought, God wasn't giving up after all.

Lily was ready to blurt out the news the minute she got home. But Mom and Dad called a family meeting almost before she and Art got in the door.

"What's this about?" Art muttered to Lily as they assembled in the family room.

"What else?" Lily said. Tessa wasn't there, so it had to be about her.

"We have only a half hour before Mom has to go pick up Tessa from therapy," Dad said. "So I'm just going to plunge right in."

"You're sending her back, right?" Joe said.

Dad shook his head. "We have a situation. I'm leaving for England on Saturday, and unfortunately your mother has been called to jury duty."

"I might not have to actually serve," Mom put in. "Jury selection is Monday, and if I'm not chosen then none of this matters."

"None of what?" Lily said. She didn't like the sound of this.

"If I'm chosen," Mom said, "I won't be getting home until about 5:00 every afternoon. With your dad in England for that time, that means there will be about two hours when no adults will be here, instead of just one hour."

*Stop!* Lily thought. *Stop before you say what I think you're going to say!*

"Art has been pretty much holding the fort since Lily's been taking riding lessons," Dad said, "and he's managed to keep Joe and Tessa from doing any bodily harm to each other."

"Then can't he keep doing it?" Lily said.

"We don't think that's fair to him," Mom said. "It's going to take all three of you—especially you and Art—to keep things from getting out of hand for that long. There are people you can call if they do—we don't expect you to handle her if she really goes off."

Both parents looked at the kids—waiting.

"Talk to us," Mom said.

"I don't see what good it's going to do for me to be there," Lily said.

"Tessa looks up to you," Mom said.

"No way! She calls me Mutant!"

"She calls me Loser," Joe said.

"I guess I got off easy," Art said. "I'm just the Band Geek. Thaaaat's original."

"It may not even happen," Mom said. "But if it does, we're counting on you guys."

Joe and Lily looked at Art. He shook his head. "How can we argue with that?"

"I can!" Joe said. "I'm the one she threatens to beat up on all the time."

"You know," Mom said to Dad, "it might be better if Joe weren't here. That would take away some of the issues."

Dad nodded. "We want her to learn to get along with you, Joe, but under these circumstances, let's just put that on hold. Where can you go after school?"

"Yeah," Art said, grinning. "Are you welcome in many houses?"

"I can go to Richie's," Joe said.

"This is *so* not fair!" Lily knew she was whining, but she couldn't stop herself. "Herbie said if I will come in Saturdays and clean the stables, I can have lessons for free — after school!"

"That's great, Lil," Mom said. "Ask him if the offer's still open in two weeks."

"It's not fair," Lily said again.

"I know, Lilliputian," Dad said. "Life so seldom is."

Lily was still furious the next morning at the Girlz' bench. She paced back and forth while the four of them watched her as if they were viewing a ping-pong match.

"It just makes me so *mad*!" she said. "I feel like my whole entire life has been ruined because of *her*. Just because *she* has the manners of a gorilla — just because *she* treats us like we're all terrorists out to get her — just because *she* hates absolutely everything — *I* have to make all these sacrifices."

The Girlz were all shaking their heads in shared anger.

"If it were happening in my house," Zooey said, "I would just — I would just leave."

"No, you would not either, Zooey," Reni said.

She went on to point out to Zooey that she'd probably get about as far as the corner, but Lily didn't hear the rest. Her eyes had been caught by a figure lurking next to the trashcan. It was Shad Shifferdecker, lazily scratching his belly so that his too-big T-shirt went up and down. He was obviously absorbing every word she was saying.

Lily had to grunt at herself. A few months earlier, she would have demanded to know what he thought he was doing, spying on them. Now she just shrugged.

"Why is Shad watching us?" Suzy whispered. She fidgeted on the bench.

"Don't worry about it," Lily said. "I've seen worse now—a *lot* worse."

Zooey's eyes popped. "You mean Tessa is worse than *Shad?*"

"Yeah," Lily said to Suzy. "She's way worse."

There was a silence. Zooey got a teary-eyed look.

"So—does this mean we just never get to see you at all except in school, Lily?"

Before Lily could answer, Kresha stood up, one sock sliding down to her ankle.

"No!" she said. "We must help Lee-lee!"

"Help how?" Reni said.

"I know about *mali desputuni*," Kresha said. "I have brothers."

"What's mali-whatever?" Reni said.

"It must be pretty awful," Suzy said. "I know her brothers."

"You do have to baby-sit them all the time, huh?" Reni said. She was warming up to the subject, sitting straight up on the bench.

"I know the way to handle them," Kresha said. "They must always play—always play. Playing keep them—what is the word?"

"Occupied?" Lily said.

"Ya!"

Lily shook her head. "That isn't going to work with Tessa. She'll either say she hates the game or she'll find some reason to beat up on somebody."

"But she's just one person," Reni said. She was nodding at Kresha. "We're five, plus Art's gonna be there. She can't take on everybody at once."

Lily considered arguing with that, but the Girlz' faces were all beginning to shine with that we-have-a-new-idea look.

"We could come to your house after school and help out with Tessa," Reni said. "It's like Kresha said, we'll keep her occupied. Kresha's had experience with those *desputuni* things."

Kresha was bobbing her head, and Reni looked as if she were ready to leave for the Robbinses' house right now. Even Suzy, although she was chewing on a fingernail, was nodding a little.

Only Zooey still looked reluctant. She was cowering against Suzy as if Lily had just pulled a snake out of her backpack.

"What, Zooey?" Reni said.

Zooey flopped her hands around. "Now don't start yelling at me, Reni," she said. "But if she's as bad as Lily says she is, I'm afraid to be around her. Kids like that pick on me—I don't know why—they just do."

"It's okay, Zooey," Lily said. "I understand, I really do."

"Then we're not going to do it?" Zooey said.

"No—*you're* not going to do it," Reni said.

"But I thought we always stuck together!"

"We do," Kresha said.

All faces were somber. Zooey buried hers against her backpack.

That afternoon, the air was warm and springtime sunny, and there was just enough of a breeze to keep the Girlz from sweating under their backpacks on the walk to Lily's house—all five of them.

Still, Lily reminded herself that Tessa could create a storm anytime. *Please don't give up, God,* she prayed to herself. *Because I'm just about to.*

When they arrived at the Robbinses' house, Art had just gotten back from picking Tessa up from school. She was sitting sullenly next to him on the front steps, curling her lip at a granola bar. She obviously hated granola bars.

"Is that her?" Suzy whispered to Lily.

"Yeah."

"What happened to her hair?" Zooey whispered.

"Would you quit whispering?" Reni said. "She's gonna think we're talking about her."

Zooey blinked. "But we are."

"Heeey, who left the henhouse door open?" Art said when they reached the steps.

"I wanted to introduce Tessa to my friends," Lily said.

Art gave her a look that clearly said, "You're kidding, right?"

Lily turned to the Girlz. "Um, Tessa—this is Zooey, and Suzy, and Kresha—"

"Weird name," Tessa said. She was looking at Kresha, who was still smiling.

Art nudged Tessa. "You should talk about having a weird name."

"My mother gave me that name!" Tessa said. She tossed the granola bar down as if to free her hands for her first punch.

"It's a great name," Art said calmly. "I wasn't putting it down."

"You said it was weird!"

"You said Kresha's name was weird—were you putting her down?"

Tessa looked back at Kresha, and Lily held her breath. Why did Art have to get into this? They were off on the wrong foot already.

"I guess not," Tessa said finally.

Kresha just grinned. Tessa swept her eyes over the rest of the Girlz. Lily wished somebody would say something, and she nudged Reni with her elbow.

"It's nice to meet you," Reni said.

"I had a colored friend once," Tessa said.

Lily could see Reni bristling.

"Waaait a minute," Art said. "Leeeet's be politically correct here." He leaned toward Tessa's ear. "That would be 'African-American.'"

"What's the difference?" Tessa said.

"You really want to know?" Reni said. "I can tell you."

"Nah," Tessa said. "I'll just call you Afro."

"Why don't you just call me Reni?"

Tension brought the breeze to a standstill. Reni locked her eyes into Tessa's, and Lily was sure she saw electricity being exchanged. To Lily's amazement, it was Tessa who broke eye contact first.

"So, Mutant," she said to Lily. "Did you bring everybody over here to stand around and stare at me?"

"No!" Kresha said. "We came to play!" She turned to Art. "You have Fris-bee?"

"We've got about six of them," he said.

"Get 'em, Art," Reni said briskly. "We want to play."

Art gave her a lopsided grin and said, "Yes, ma'am."

"I'm going to go in and make us some snacks," Zooey whispered when Art had headed for the garage. She escaped into the house.

"So how do you play Frisbee?" Tessa said.

Lily shrugged. "You just throw it to each other."

"How do you win?"

"You don't," Reni said.

"Sounds boring," Tessa said. "I ain't playin' no lame game."

"There's ways you can win."

Lily gaped at Suzy, who until now hadn't opened her mouth.

"Hey," Tessa said. "She talks."

"We play cutthroat at our house," Suzy said. "My father showed us."

To Lily's amazement, Suzy went on to explain the rules of cutthroat Frisbee, and to her further amazement, Tessa didn't yell, "That's so stupid!" or "I hate it!"

When Art produced several Frisbees and they started the game, with Art watching like a line judge from the front steps, Lily thought she couldn't be any more amazed. Reni was her usual driven self, taking charge of the Frisbee right away and making a direct toss to the first goal. Suzy, who had a competitive streak hidden under her shyness, went after it by hurling herself through the air. Tessa was, for once, caught off guard, but it took her only a few minutes to get into the thick of it. Suzy and Reni made it so hard for her to get the Frisbee — except for a few easy throws to keep her from getting frustrated — that she had to concentrate very hard. It didn't seem to occur to her to aim one right at someone's head.

But Lily's ultimate amazement came when she looked up to see Shad Shifferdecker sauntering into her yard, hands in his baggy pockets, chewing on a toothpick.

"Is that your boyfriend?" Art said to Lily.

"Uh, no-o. Hello!"

"That's Shad Shifferdecker," Zooey whispered. She had just stepped out onto the porch with a tray of mini-pizzas and was already white-faced.

Art looked up at her, amused. "Should we call 9-1-1?"

By then Shad had put himself between Reni and Tessa and jumped up and caught the Frisbee. He held it above Tessa's head as she grabbed for it. Since there were about four feet between her fingertips and the Frisbee, it was, of course, pointless. In true Tessa fashion, however, she kept leaping.

"Give me that!" she said. "You're not even in the game!"

"Who says, girlfriend?" Shad said.

"Oh," Art said to Lily. "He's *Tessa's* boyfriend."

"He's going to be Tessa's next victim if he doesn't knock it off," Lily said.

"Make him go home, Art," Zooey said, still whispering.

"Leeet's give it a few," Art said. "I think Tessa might've met her match."

Art, it appeared, was right. Shad did let go of the Frisbee, sailing it to Suzy. Then he jumped in front of Tessa, blocking her next grab for it. When she shouted, "Not fair!" Shad picked her up, both hands on her waist, and lifted her high enough to grab Suzy's next expert high-spin. Tessa stopped shouting.

For the next thirty minutes, it was like that — Shad, Suzy, and Reni keeping the Frisbee from her one minute and then helping her to catch it the next. Shad ran with her up on his shoulders to get a high one and slid with her on his back to get a grounder before it hit the grass.

Lily was laughing so hard it took her several minutes to realize that Tessa was laughing too — for the first time since she'd come.

Reni pooped out after awhile, and Zooey quickly called out, "Pizza!"

Tessa started in with, "What are these puny little things? I want real pizza."

"So don't eat it then," Shad said. "Can I have her piece?"

"No!" Tessa said and stuffed a whole one in her mouth.

Then Art announced that it was time for Tessa to get started on her homework.

"This is where I check out," Shad said. "Later."

Tessa scowled as he sauntered off. "Is everybody else gonna leave now too, and I have to be all by myself?"

Lily was stunned.

"No," Reni said. "We'll help ya with your homework. We're all A students."

"Except for me," Zooey said.

"What are you, a retard?"

There was a group gasp. Lily was about to lash out at Tessa, but Art cut in with, "You want us to start calling *you* that because your grades are, shall we say, less than outstanding?"

"You better not!"

"Then where do you get off saying stuff like that to other people?"

"She'd say it to me if I gave her the chance!"

Zooey was shaking her head. "I wouldn't call you that, because I *know* what it's like to be the dumbest kid in the class."

"Come on," Art said to Tessa. "Let's hit the books."

When they were all spread out at the dining room table, with Kresha and Suzy on the floor because there wasn't enough room for six binders, six textbooks, and six sets of elbows on the tabletop, Reni said, "So what subject do you need help with? If it's English, Lily can help you. Math — Suzy's a whiz. And if it's science, Kresha's your girl —"

But it was Zooey who Tessa turned to. "Do you hate math?" she said.

"Yes!" Zooey said. "I wish there was a law against it!"

"You flunking it?"

"No."

"How come?"

"Because." Zooey hesitated. "I took some special classes," she said carefully, "and they helped me learn some tricks. Now I make, like, B's and C's in it."

Tessa pulled a slightly wrinkled paper out of her backpack and slapped it down on the table. "Help me with this," she said.

The rest of the Girlz gaped at Lily, but Zooey sat down next to Tessa and started in. Lily just shrugged — and then prayed that Zooey wouldn't end up with a pencil stuck in her ear or something.

By the time Mom got home, all the Girlz had their homework done. And so did Tessa. Lily thought Zooey looked as if she had just delivered a baby or something.

But Lily focused her attention on Mom. *We got through this day,* she thought. *Is this the last one? God — please let it be the last one.*

"So — what's the verdict, Mom?" Art said. He grinned and added, "Yuck, yuck, yuck."

"Guilty," Mom said, raising her hand. "I'm on the jury starting Monday."

She looked firmly from Lily to Art, as if to make sure neither of them planned to fall to the floor begging. Tessa was watching her.

"What's the big deal?" Tessa said. "We all play Frisbee after school with that Shad-dude, and Zoology helps me with my homework, and we eat pizza." She shrugged—like it was all settled.

"Zoology?" Zooey said. She giggled. "Is that me?"

"It could work, y'know," Reni said. "It would be like having Girlz Only here. I wouldn't get to take riding lessons, though, because I have to do violin at least two days a week."

*No!* Lily wanted to scream. *Tessa isn't part of Girlz Only!*

But no one else seemed to think of that. As they left, the Girlz reassured Lily that they had had a great time and this was going to be fun. Lily couldn't agree.

Mom took Lily aside later and thanked her for making Tessa feel accepted. She also told her that the next day, Tessa had therapy and Art was taking her, so Lily could go take her riding lesson. He could take her by after he dropped Tessa off.

"You lucked out," Mom said.

But when Lily climbed into bed that night with Otto and her journal, she didn't feel particularly lucky. Sure, things had gone better with Tessa than she'd dared hope they would, but could they keep that up for two weeks?

*I know, I know,* she wrote. *You don't give up on us. But—no offense, God—I feel like I want to give up about half the time these days.*

She closed her journal and tossed her gel pen across the bed. She felt like giving up writing in it right now.

She glared at the floor. And who could even think about God with Tessa carrying on her nightly jam session on the wall?

# Chapter 11

The next afternoon, Herbie was surprised to see Lily, but he grinned his gap-toothed grin and told her Jake was ready to be saddled up. For the first time, she put the saddle on all by herself, with a little help on the lifting from Georgie. When Herbie checked it, he said it was perfect.

Still, as she mounted Big Jake, Lily felt out of sorts. This was fine for today, but tomorrow she'd be back with Tessa. And she missed Reni.

She reached for the reins Herbie was holding, but he didn't give them to her right away.

"What's on your mind today, Lily-girl?" he said "You gave me this nice surprise today, and now you've got that long face again."

Lily sighed and ran her finger across the saddle horn. "It's about the reason I can come only on Saturday for the next two weeks. It's that new girl who's living at our house."

"You have to babysit her, you said."

"It's more than that. See, she has — well, issues — and it takes, like, six people to handle her. And I hate it because then I don't get to come here."

Herbie tipped his hat back with one finger to look at her. "So why don't you bring her with you?"

Lily stared. "You mean, to the Double H?"

"Why not? You worked hard enough on Saturday for two people."

Lily shook her head firmly. "You don't want her here, Herbie. She's totally out of control. She calls people names, and she spits and kicks when she doesn't get her way. She gave my brother Joe a bloody nose the first day she was at our house!"

"Can't be any worse than training a horse."

Lily ran her hand down Big Jake's mane. "None of your horses ever behaves like her."

"That's not what's really bothering you," Herbie said.

Lily stared miserably at her hands as they folded into Big Jake's coarse hair. "You'd have to spend the whole time dealing with her. I wouldn't even get a decent lesson. I just want one thing that I don't have to change around or give up because of her." She could feel her throat closing. "I guess that's selfish."

"I guess that's human. And don't you worry. You earn your lessons, and you'll get them. Just bring her along." He patted Big Jake on the cheek. "You think about it while you're riding. Let's put him through his paces."

Lily did think about it, more than she thought about the wind in her hair or the wonderful, floating way Big Jake felt under her when they ran. She kept coming back to the same conclusion — she wanted just one thing that could be hers and hers alone.

It was nearly 6:30 when Mom got home that evening. Joe was home, and at 5:00 Art had made a deal with Lily that if she dealt with Tessa, he would keep Joe out of their hair. Lily made macaroni and cheese—which Tessa said she hated but ate anyway—and then, having had a stroke of genius, she put Tessa on the phone with Zooey so they could do Tessa's homework. Zooey loved to talk on the phone anyway.

Mom gave an approving but weary smile when she saw Tessa with the receiver nestled in her neck, writing down numbers on a paper and saying, "Uh-huh. I get it."

"Bless you, Lil," Mom said. "I never meant for you to have to do all this—but things happen. I owe you."

"This thing is beeping in my ear," Tessa said, holding the phone away from her and glaring at it.

"That's call waiting," Mom said. She took the phone from Tessa and punched a button. "Hello?" she said. "Oh, Mr. Hajek, how ya doin'?"

"Who's Mr. Hajek?" Tessa said to Lily.

"My riding teacher," Lily said. She was watching intently as her mother listened and nodded.

"What's he callin' here for? Did you get in trouble today?"

"No!" Lily said. "Would you just be quiet—it's none of your business!"

Mom frowned at Lily, even as she said into the phone. "That is so generous of you. Are you sure you want to do this? You may not know what you're getting into." She paused and frowned more deeply in Lily's direction. "I'm sure she did. Well, if you're serious, I'll have my son drop both of them off day after tomorrow. But anytime you want to change your mind, just let me know."

Lily stared in disbelief as her mother said good-bye to Herbie.

"Drop both of us off where?" Tessa said.

"At the riding stables. Mr. Hajek says you can come with Lily while she has her lessons."

Tessa snorted. "And stand around in horse poop the whole time?"

"Yes!" Lily said. "Because that's right where you belong—because no matter what anybody tries to do for you—you just act evil and say horrible things! So yeah—you can just stand in horse poop for all I care!"

"Lilianna," Mom said.

Lily didn't wait to hear more. She stormed out of the kitchen and somehow got to her room, where she threw herself face down on her bed and cried herself to sleep.

The next morning, Mom told her she understood how Lily felt, but she would appreciate it if there were no more outbursts like that. It reinforced Tessa's behavior, whatever that meant.

Lily would rather she had out and out yelled at her and grounded her for life. Mom just seemed too tired to do much of anything.

After school, the Girlz came over as they'd promised. Personally, Lily told herself, she could care less whether Tessa got her homework done or pitched a fit.

"No offense, Lily," Zooey said as they were walking home, "but I don't think Tessa's that bad."

"You wouldn't," Reni said. "She actually likes you."

Zooey's face took on a look of wonderful surprise. "She does?" she said. "You think she does?"

*Like that's life's desire,* Lily thought.

They played Frisbee again that day, with some variations Suzy came up with when Tessa looked like she was getting bored. All boredom left for good when Shad showed up. Lily hadn't had time to figure that one out. He stayed until Art called for homework.

When they got into the dining room, Tessa's backpack was already on the table where she'd dropped it. There was also a large poster of a black horse, shiny and stately.

Lily went straight to it. "What's this?" she said. "This is a gorgeous horse. I bet it's a thoroughbred."

"It's mine," Tessa said. "So don't get any ideas."

"Where'd you get it?" Reni said.

"I told my teacher I was gonna start horseback riding," Tessa said, "and she took it off the wall and give it to me."

"Nuh-uh!" Reni said.

"You callin' me a liar?"

"Re-laaax," Art said.

Tessa looked at Lily. "You said I didn't appreciate anything anybody did for me." She poked a finger at the poster. "I appreciated this. I'm hanging it up in my room."

She did, that very night. At least, that was what Mom told Lily. Lily didn't go down to look at it.

"If she's going to throw things up in my face like that, forget her," Lily told Otto. "She doesn't really like that poster. She's just doing this because she thinks I want it." Lily gave a sniff and then looked, shamefaced, at Otto. "I do want it. It's nicer than mine."

Just then the banging commenced. Otto jumped down from the bed and went to the door, where he barked and clawed until Lily picked him up and fed him a dog treat. She smiled to herself. At least *he* wasn't being won over by Tessa.

But smiles became fewer and farther between the next day as Lily thought more and more about the afternoon riding lesson.

*I love riding,* she thought mournfully as she waited for Art to pick her up. *Now she's going to ruin that too.*

The only thing that kept Lily from telling Art to forget it was Art's announcement that since she and Tessa were going to be at the stables for a while, he was going to get in a jam session with his jazz group. He said he was going into withdrawal.

"At least you don't have to take *her* with you," Lily told him.

He looked sympathetic as he said to her, "Tough break, Lil."

They picked up Tessa, who asked questions all the way to the Double H.

"How many horses they got?"

"Are any of them that thoroughbred thing you were talking about?"

"What about this Hajek guy — he's not a loser, is he?"

Lily answered them all with grunts.

Herbie was waiting at the open end of the stable, one booted foot crossed over the other. He was in his usual cowboy attire.

"Is he for real?" Tessa said.

"Yes," Lily said tightly. "He's the most real person I know right now."

"I'd watch myself," Art said to Tessa as she climbed out of the car. "The dude is wearing spurs."

"This is Tessa," Lily said to Herbie. She jerked her chin at Tessa. "This is Herbie."

"How you doing, Little Girlie?" Herbie said, tipping his hat slightly.

Lily cringed. Tessa was going to have a field day with that.

To her surprise, Tessa said, "Fine. How you doin', Little Mannie?"

Herbie chuckled. "You want to go in and see the horses?"

He pointed inside, and Tessa took off. Lily craned her neck to watch. She didn't want Tessa to try to shove something up one of their noses or something.

"So far so good," Herbie said to Lily. "Now you need to concentrate on your riding and leave Little Girlie to me."

"I'll try," Lily said.

She was feeling a little relieved as she walked into the stable—until she saw Tessa.

She had her face resting on Big Jake's long nose, her eyes closed as she stroked his cheek.

"This horse digs me," she said to Herbie. "This is the one I wanna ride."

Lily took a deep breath. She knew if she didn't get a hold of herself right away, there was going to be worse than an outburst. Herbie, though, didn't waste a minute.

"Who said you were going to ride?" he said to Tessa. "Lily-girl works for lessons. If you want lessons, you're going to have to prove yourself around here."

*Here comes the standing in horse poop part,* Lily thought. *Let the screaming begin.*

"Prove myself how?" Tessa said.

Herbie picked up a flat-headed shovel and handed it to her. "You start at the bottom and work your way up. Every horse in here has left you a little present that needs to be shoveled up."

Tessa shifted her eyes to Lily. "Did she ever have to shovel it?"

"By the pile," Herbie said.

Tessa shrugged. "No big deal. Where do I put it?"

Lily could only stare until Herbie gave her a little nudge. "You saddle up Big Jake while I show Little Girlie the ropes," he said.

Lily and Georgie had never saddled her horse as fast as she did that day. She wanted it done in case Tessa proved herself in record time and was ready for lessons before she and Big Jake could get out of the stall.

Herbie joined her outside and mounted Jiminy beside her. "She's in good hands with Georgie, Lily-girl. Let's ride."

It may have been Lily's best lesson yet. She and Big Jake were starting to move like they were one being, and this time Lily forgot about everything but him and the way she was riding. She didn't even think about Tessa.

When she did, it was on the way back to the stable to groom Big Jake. *I bet she gave Georgie a fit,* she thought. *After about two shovels full.*

But when she led an unsaddled Jake to his stall, Tessa was sweeping it in a manner resembling the Tasmanian devil.

"It's ready," she said to Lily. "Now don't mess it up."

She propped up the broom and hung on the stall's half door. "What are you gonna do now?" she said.

"Groom," Lily said.

"What for?"

"Because he's not a cat," Lily said. "It's not like he can groom himself."

She picked up a stiff brush and ran it down Big Jake's side, crooning softly as she worked.

"What's that?" Tessa said. She grunted. "Or do you even know?"

"Of course I know," Lily said. "I'm brushing to get all the dust off of him and make his coat shine."

"Dude," Tessa said. "It works. Look at that."

Lily resisted the urge to stare at her. They had had a decent conversation—and Tessa didn't look as if she were working up to anything.

"You want to know what else I'm doing?" Lily said.

"I ain't got nothin' else to do," Tessa said. "Go for it."

So Lily described everything she was doing as she brushed and combed and rubbed. Tessa swung on the door and listened until Big Jake was settled in with water and a bucket of sweet feed and a blanket over his back.

"I'm surprised you don't give him a stuffed animal," Tessa said.

"No," Lily said. "I already gave my best one to you."

Tessa seemed a little surprised, though she immediately hid it in a rubber-mouthed smirk. "The panda was your favorite, huh?"

"Yeah," Lily said.

Tessa shrugged. "Too bad," she said.

It left a bad aftertaste on what had been a not-too-bad afternoon.

# Chapter 12

But as the next few days and then the weekend went by, even the aftertaste began to fade. Calmer days began to unfold.

Tessa still had to be dragged out of bed in the morning—especially Sunday—and she still hammered on the wall with her feet at night until she fell asleep. And she still referred to Lily as Mutant and Joe as Loser.

But she only glared at Joe across the dinner table. She didn't threaten to tear off any of his limbs. Not seeing him most of the time definitely helped.

She got her homework done every afternoon, though Lily told Art that from the looks of it, she probably still wasn't passing.

The Frisbee games became more complex and more competitive, due in large part to Suzy and Shad. Nobody questioned Shad's presence anymore, although one day Tessa asked him, "How come you never come in and do homework?"

Lily knew the answer to that one. She'd learned last fall when they were in a play together that Shad had a thing called dyslexia, which made it hard for him to read. Strangely, she didn't want Tessa embarrassing him.

"I'm, like, dumb," Shad said with a careless shrug.

"So's Zoology," Tessa said. "But she's helpin' me. Get her to help you."

Reni looked at Lily and pressed her lips together so that her dimples deepened into her cheeks. It was hard for Lily not to laugh too. Zooey and Shad? Zooey would faint dead away. As it was, Zooey was looking a little pasty.

"I don't got my stuff with me," Shad said.

"Bring it tomorrow," Tessa said. "No, the next day. We got riding lessons tomorrow."

*We don't,* Lily thought. *I do.*

And then she let the thought go. Tessa was being pretty okay. And Herbie had already said there would be no lessons until Tessa had proven herself. And besides, even if Tessa did get lessons, it wouldn't be with Lily and it wouldn't be on Big Jake. So why get all in a knot about it? Maybe she should hang in there with God a little longer.

Besides all of *that,* tomorrow was Friday, hopefully the last day Mom had to do jury duty. And Dad would be home Saturday — so the after-school Tessa watch was over. She wouldn't be coming to the stables with Lily anymore anyway.

Lily was light-hearted the next afternoon when she and Tessa piled out of Ruby Sue and raced each other to the stables.

Lily started saddling up Big Jake right away and had it half done when Herbie strolled in. Tessa greeted him with the shovel in her hand.

"Ain't I proved myself already?" she said.

"You pitched hay yet?" Herbie said.

"Four times."

"Filled feed buckets?"

"Yep."

"Cleaned leather?"

"You seen me doin' it!"

Lily watched Herbie over Big Jake's back. He couldn't be considering lessons, could he?

And then Lily shook her head. *It's okay,* she told herself. *She still won't be with me.*

But somehow, that didn't feel especially happy. Snippets of the past week danced in Lily's head. Tessa swinging on the stall gate while Lily lectured her on horse grooming. Tessa walking beside Lily and Big Jake the minute they returned from their lesson, going straight to the stable with them. Tessa sitting on the Round Pen fence watching Lily learn a new technique, thumping her feet happily against the bars.

Even Tessa triumphantly snatching M&Ms from Zooey because she'd gotten all the three times tables right—and tackling Shad on the lawn but not pounding on him. Not to mention interrogating all the Girlz at 5:00 to make sure they were coming back the next time.

"Well, Little Girlie," she heard Herbie say. "Let's see if we can't put you on Gretchen and have Georgie get you started."

"It's okay," Lily whispered to herself. Then she stood on tiptoes and said, "That'll be cool, Tessa. Kresha rode Gretchen, and she said she was a nice horse."

"Nah," Tessa said. She appeared on the other side of Big Jake. "I wanna ride this one."

Lily looked around wildly for Herbie, who was leaning his forearms on the stall gate.

"You're not ready for that, Little Girlie. Today, it's Gretchen or nothing."

"Not fair," Tessa said.

"Yeah, yeah," Herbie said. "Let's go find Georgie."

Lily sagged against Big Jake for a minute when they were gone. Jake turned his head to try and look at her.

"It's okay, baby," Lily said as she hugged his neck and smelled his sweet-feed breath. "It's just you and me."

That day, Herbie taught Lily how to gallop.

"Swing your heels out and bring them in," he told her. "Big Jake loves to go — if you'll remember."

Lily couldn't wait to feel her hair streaming out behind her, medieval maiden style. But galloping was the most difficult thing she'd tried yet. She was only just beginning to get her ups and downs coordinated with Big Jake's ups and downs when time was up.

"It'll come easier next week," Herbie said as they ambled toward the stables. He glanced at Lily sideways. "And you'll be here without the Little Girlie."

"Yeah," Lily said.

"It hasn't been so bad," Herbie said.

"No," Lily said. "It hasn't."

She wondered then how Tessa's lesson had gone.

*In a way I hope she didn't like it too much,* Lily thought. *Because she doesn't get to come back any more.*

"Now there's a long face," Herbie said, pointing.

Lily looked to see Tessa sitting on the low fence just outside the stable, feet banging the rails the way they did on the walls at night.

Lily slid off of Big Jake and went to her.

"What's going on?" she said. "You didn't get hurt, did you?"

"No," Tessa said. She punched her chin up into the air, but her eyes were droopy, and no amount of pretending she didn't care could give them their usual angry gleam.

"So what happened?" Lily said.

"Nothin' happened."

"Something had to happen, or you wouldn't look so bummed out."

"She's not lying," Georgie said from the stable door. "I couldn't get her to stay on the horse. Scared to death."

Lily stared at Tessa. "No, you were not!"

"Just leave me alone, okay?" Tessa said.

She jumped down from the fence and was about to bolt when Herbie caught her and put his arm around her. Usually Tessa balked at hugging, but Lily suspected Herbie had a pretty strong hold on her.

"Nothing to be ashamed of," he said. "A horse is a big animal. I think Lily-girl was a little skittish herself at first."

He looked at Lily.

"Yeah—I guess I was," Lily said slowly. It was hard to let the words come out. "It seemed like a long way to the ground, and I was sure I was gonna break my neck." She looked at Tessa, who was watching her like an FBI agent. "And you're even littler than me," Lily said. "I bet it looked like miles down to you."

Tessa shrugged, but she didn't deny it.

"I have an idea," Herbie said. "But, now, Lily-girl, if you don't like it, you don't have to do it."

Lily was already nodding. "She can ride with me—on Big Jake. I won't let you fall, Tessa."

Tessa looked as if she were being torn in half. Lily saw it as a clear case of wanting to ride so badly she could taste it—and being so scared, she could taste that too.

"Okay," Lily said. "I'll get on first so you don't have to be up there by yourself even for a second. Then you'll get on in front of me, and we'll go real slow. If you want to get off, we just stop and you get down."

Tessa stopped banging her feet and sat there watching one of them wiggle at the ankle. "You gonna tell everybody I couldn't do it by myself?"

"No," Lily said. "And maybe you will do it by yourself. Maybe after you ride with me a little, you won't be so scared, and I'll get off and Herbie'll lead you."

"You gonna call me Wimp from now on?" Tessa said.

"You're the one who gives everybody a nickname that hurts their feelings," Lily said. "Not me."

Lily felt a twinge of guilt the minute those words were out of her mouth. She *had* referred to Tessa as Devil Child before. But it occurred to her now that she hadn't even thought that in about a week and a half.

"Okay," Tessa said. "Get on."

Lily had a different feeling as she mounted Big Jake this time. He had taught her, and she had taught him. Now together they were going to teach Tessa. It was as if they were connected at the heart. *Or something like that,* she thought.

Once she was settled in the saddle, she leaned down close to Big Jake's ear. It twitched as she whispered to him, "Be really gentle with her. She's kinda scared. We gotta teach her."

Below, Herbie helped Tessa put her foot into the stirrup and gave her a boost. She settled easily into the saddle in front of Lily. But the minute Herbie let go of her and she uncurled her fingers from around his sleeve, she grabbed Lily's wrist as Lily reached around her to take hold of the reins. Jake did a little sidestep.

's he doing?" Tessa said. Her voice was shrill.

ust getting used to us being on him," Lily said. "I won't tell until you're ready."

"Can I hang onto you?" Tessa said.

"Hang onto her leg," Herbie said. "She needs her hands free."

Tessa did a quick switch from fingers grasping Lily's wrist to fingers clenching a fold in Lily's jeans on either side. If she hung on any tighter, Lily was sure she'd be grabbing skin.

"You can trust Lily-girl," Herbie said to Tessa. "And you're not going to go fast, so I'll be walking right here beside you girlies. Got it?"

Tessa gave a stiff nod, as if her neck were frozen.

"You ready?" Lily said.

There was another nod. Lily picked up the reins and said softly to Big Jake, "Let's go, boy."

It was as if Big Jake knew he had fragile cargo on board. He stepped forward, gently moving in the slow, straight line Lily guided him in.

"He's moving," Tessa said, barely opening her lips. "*We're* moving."

"See how fun it is?" Lily said. She glanced down at the fingers that were practically squeezing the dye out of her jeans. "Herbie taught me it's even more fun if you relax."

Tessa didn't loosen her fingers much, but she did slowly, inch by inch, lean back so that she was pressed against Lily. Lily's chest went warm.

They rocked along for a few minutes, Big Jake bobbing his head up and down, Herbie walking beside them grinning. Tessa finally uncurled her fingers.

"Can you make him turn?" Tessa said.

"Sure," Lily said. She guided Big Jake to the right, let him walk a few paces, and then turned him to the left.

"That rocks!" Tessa said. "Can I try it?"

Lily looked down at Herbie. He nodded.

Lily took one of Tessa's hands and put it on the rein. "Hold onto it with me," she said. "And just pull it real easy this way."

Magically, Tessa did exactly as she said. Big Jake obediently turned to the right.

"I'm doin' it, Lily!" Tessa cried. "I'm riding a horse!"

Then she looked over her shoulder at Lily, and she smiled.

There was no need for Lily to keep her mouth shut about Tessa's being afraid of riding. Tessa told the entire story at the dinner table that night, complete with shouts of "It rocked!" and "Dude—I'm doin' that again!"

Lily and Mom exchanged glances over that one.

Mom, who looked more rested already, even though the trial had been over for only two hours, twitched her mouth at Tessa.

"We ought to celebrate," she said. "That's a win for you."

"Blizzard at Dairy Queen," Tessa said without hesitation.

"Nah, let's go to Friendly's," Joe said. "Their stuff's better."

Tessa's face clouded over as she looked at Joe. "It's just gonna be me and her," she said, jerking her head toward Mom. Then she squinted her green eyes, as if she were considering something seriously. "No," she said, "It's gonna be just me and her—and Lily."

Joe went into a string of "that's not fair" with Mom. Lily sat back and closed her eyes.

*She called me Lily,* she thought. *She's called me Lily twice now, and not Mutant. And she wants me to come with her and Mom.*

Why, she wondered, did that feel good? Really good.

The next day Mom had to go the airport to pick up Dad, and Art was going to be running around like a taxi driver, taking Joe to baseball practice, Lily to the Double H, and then getting himself to a saxophone lesson. Mom poked her head into Lily's room as she was putting on the red boots.

"Lil," Mom said. "I hate to do this to you, but I'm going to need to send Tessa with you just one more time. I'd take her to the airport with me, but your Dad and I need that hour on the ride home to reconnect. I know we've dumped a lot on you—"

"Mom," Lily said, "don't worry about it. It's okay. She can come."

Mom looked startled. "You sure?" she said.

Lily shrugged. "Yeah—it's fine. She's never pitched one of her fits there or anything."

Mom's mouth twitched. "I'm not worried about her—I'm thinking about you. What about you wanting to have something that was just yours?"

*Yeah, what about that?* Lily thought. And then she realized something. "I do have it," she said.

She wanted to explain, but Mom was already headed for the door.

"Lil," she said, "you continue to amaze me. See you this afternoon."

Lily's and Tessa's morning at the stables was filled with shoveling and pitching and watering and having homemade cranberry muffins with Herbie and Georgie—compliments of Georgie's wife. Tessa, Lily discovered, had never had cranberries before, and she dissected her muffin to dig one out and, all suspicion, put it in her mouth.

"That rocks!" she said.

Herbie shook his head and grinned. "You two girlies are something else. I never saw two kids get so excited about the smallest things."

*You're saying Tessa and I are alike?* Lily thought. *Yikes!*

When she and Tessa got home at lunchtime, Dad was there. Lily hurled herself at him and got a pick-up hug, the kind where her feet left the ground. Tessa wasn't that enthusiastic, but she did let Dad put his arm around her shoulder without yanking herself away as if he were some kind of reptile.

After lunch, Dad invited Lily to come into his study. His blue eyes looked misty.

"I am so proud of you, Lilliputian," he said. "Tessa has come miles while I've been gone, and I know most of that is because of you and Art and your friends." His eyes twinkled. "I hear even old Shad Shifferdecker has been lending a hand."

"Yeah," Lily said. "Who woulda thought, huh?"

"I think the lion's share of it has been you, though. I can see the way Tessa looks at you."

"It's a little creepy," Lily said.

"I don't think it's creepy at all. I think she looks up to you. She wants to be like you." Dad rubbed his hand on Lily's arm. "And I don't blame her. You're a wonderful role model. I think I want to be like you when I grow up too."

"Daaad," Lily said.

"I'm serious," Dad said. He sat back in his chair, lacing his fingers over his tummy. "I'm having to do a lot of growing in a very short time right now—your mother too. We thought we were ready for Tessa, even after we met her and knew she was going to be a handful."

"You went to all those classes and everything," Lily said.

"We went to the classes, read the books, prayed. We thought we were set." He shook his head sadly. "The poor little thing is so plagued with the things that have happened to her, she has more problems than either of us could have imagined. We weren't ready. We weren't even close to being ready — and that made things awfully hard for you and your brothers. We hadn't prepared you properly. We thought we could just slowly weave her into the family."

"Weave?" Lily said. "I think she tore a hole in it!"

Dad grinned. "That she did! But it looks to me as if you kids have rewoven it and made a new design." He stopped and looked closely at Lily. "I'm not being too abstract, am I? You're following this?"

"I think so," Lily said. "Everything's different, but some of it's not that bad."

"For the short time she's been here," Dad said, "I think that's a miracle."

"I've been praying," Lily said. "But, Dad, I haven't been, like, this angel—"

"The slate is clean, Lilliputian. In fact, we want to honor you."

"I'm gonna get a plaque or something?"

"No. We want you to continue your riding lessons three days a week. We'll pay for them. And you do not have to take Tessa. We're going to try to find her some activities that's she's interested in."

"She's interested in horses," Lily heard herself saying. "You should see her at the stables—"

"The stables are your territory," Dad said. "That gives you two days to stay with Tessa and two for Art. I'll come home early on Fridays." He reached over and put his hand on Lily's. "You just go and enjoy. You deserve it."

Lily called all the Girlz and told them. When she delivered the news to Reni, there was a funny pause.

"What?" Lily said.

"You don't sound all happy about it," Reni said.

"I'm happy, sort of," Lily said. "It's just—I haven't minded her being there that much. And she's even calling me Lily now."

"You're starting to like her," Reni said. "Which is cool, because now we can all admit to you that we like her too."

"All the Girlz?" Lily said.

"Yeah, especially Zooey. Now that she's Teacher of the Year."

"Yikes," Lily said—in a very un-yikes voice.

On Sunday after church, the Robbinses all went bike riding down by the river. Mom surprised Tessa with a used bike she bought for her that was in good shape, and she got right on it and took off. There had to be a discussion about that.

At one point, as Tessa was riding beside Lily—where she stayed for most of the ride—she said, "This is pretty boring after you been on a horse, huh?"

"Yeah," Lily said. "I keep wondering where the reins are."

"Man," Tessa said. "I can't wait to ride again."

Lily's chest got heavy. *Haven't Mom and Dad told her yet? Are they thinking I'm gonna tell her? No way!* She didn't have a chance to ask them in the Sunday night/Monday morning rush of getting ready for the week. She wrote about it in her talking-to-God journal though.

*God—just don't let Tessa's feelings be too hurt, okay? I don't know what bad stuff she's been through, but I kinda think she's had enough. I mean, you're God, so you know what you're doing. Just— please—think about it, would you? Just—don't give up on her.*

It weighed on Lily's mind all day Monday — how Tessa was going to feel about not going to the stables with her.

"Come on, Lil," Reni said at lunch. "At least you get to ride by yourself."

"Yeah," Lily said. But even that didn't shimmer in her mind.

And when Art picked her up that afternoon, he had even worse news.

"I'm going to pick up Tessa, then take you to the stables, and then I'm taking her with me to the music store over in Rancocas."

"No!" Lily said.

"It'll be fiiine," Art said. "I don't think she's going to bash a trumpet over somebody's head. I think she's past that now."

"I don't want her sitting here in the car while I go into the stables! That's mean! That's like throwing it in her face!"

"Look, she's got to understand that we all have our thing. Tomorrow Mom's taking her to karate class to see if she likes that."

"Does she at least know she's not going with me?"

Art shrugged. "I don't know. I guess so."

He pulled into the driveway in front of Cedar Hills Elementary, where Tessa was waiting — knocking her heel against a pole, over and over.

"I think you have your answer," Art said.

Tessa opened Ruby Sue's rear door and threw her backpack in. She climbed in after it and slammed the door.

"It didn't go well today, huh?" Art said.

"Shut up, Band Geek," Tessa said.

Lily's mouth went dry. She turned around in the seat as Art pulled away from the school.

"Mom and Dad told you, huh?"

Tessa didn't answer. She didn't have to. The glint in her eyes spoke like a set of encyclopedias.

"It wasn't my idea," Lily said. "They're the ones who said you should have an activity of your own—not me."

"You're a liar, Mutant. Just don't talk to me, because all you do is lie."

"I don't!" Lily said. She got up on her knees, the seatbelt around her rear end. "You have to believe me—if it were up to me—"

"Blah blah blah blah!" Tessa shouted. She put her hands over her ears and kept it up—"Blah blah blah blah."

"Sit down, Lil," Art said, in a Mom-calm voice. "You can't reason with her now. Just sit down."

By the time they got to the stables, Tessa was getting hoarse, but she didn't stop, even as Lily got out of the car.

"I'm sorry!" Lily shouted over her.

That only made the blah-blahs louder.

Lily felt as if her chest were going to break open. She turned and walked toward the stables, Tessa's anger ringing in her ears.

*I don't even blame her,* Lily thought. *I feel like screaming too. Okay, then, don't let her go. Keep her here and explain to Mom and Dad later.*

She whirled around, already running for the car. But Art was too far down the drive to hear her, and Ruby Sue kept kicking up retreating dust no matter how loudly Lily shouted or how fast she ran after her.

Tessa turned around just as Lily began to give up and slow down. She'd stopped shouting. Her eyes were still angry as she looked at Lily through the rear window. But there was something else in them too.

It was tears.

Lily rode listlessly that afternoon and even asked Herbie if she could quit early and just sit with Big Jake in the stall.

"You missing your little sister?" he said.

"She's not my sister," Lily said automatically. Then she looked up at Herbie, who was watching her. "I guess she is, really."

"As much alike as you two are, of course she is."

Lily had to nod. "She ought to be here with me."

"Then maybe you ought to take care of that, Lily-girl," Herbie said.

After that, Lily couldn't wait to get home. As soon as she slid into the front seat of Ruby Sue, she said to Art, "How's Tessa?"

"We didn't go to the music store," he said. "Thaaaaat was a no-brainer. She wouldn't do anything I told her to. She threw a whole plate of cheese and tortilla chips on the floor." Art shook his head. "When Mom came home, she finally had to put her in her room by her-self. She banged the wall for a while, and then she finally shut up."

"I know what's wrong with her," Lily said. "I can fix it."

"Good luck," was all Art said.

The minute she was in the house, Lily went straight for her room to dump her stuff off before she went in to see Tessa. She threw open her door, head full of all that she was going to say to her sister—but what she saw froze her in the doorway.

There was China, back on her bed—with a gash cut right down his middle.

# Chapter 14

Lily felt like her own chest was going to split open as she went to the panda and took him in her arms. When she pulled away, there was stuffing on the front of her shirt.

"I hate that she did this to you!" she said to China. "She didn't even give me a chance to explain!"

Otto crawled out from under the bed and jumped up beside China. He flattened himself on the bedspread, ears down as if Lily had just scolded him.

"Otto, did she do it in here? Did you see her do it?"

Otto whined and tried to get flatter. Lily fingered his ear and brought back a sticky hand.

"What is *this*?" she said. She sniffed her finger, and her nose filled with the familiar aroma of Pledge.

"She sprayed you?" Lily cried. "Oh, Otto! I'm so sorry!"

Otto whined louder and more pitifully as Lily scooped him up against her and clutched him and China as if Tessa were going to burst in any minute, a spray can in one hand and a knife in the other.

"She threatened to crush your skull once," she said to Otto. "But I thought she was over that. She must have been really mad."

And then another thought came, like a whisper. *She must be really hurt.*

"She was out of it," Lily said to the both of them. "She didn't even know what she was doing, I bet."

Otto wriggled away and retreated under the bed. Lily gave China another squeeze. "I'll be back to take care of your tummy," she said.

Feeling as if she might throw up any minute, Lily hurried down the stairs to Tessa's room and knocked on the door. There was no answer, not even a "Go away, Mutant."

Lily turned the knob and pushed the door open — slowly, in case Tessa really was armed.

But she wasn't in the room, even when Lily checked the closet. Lily felt deflated, and she sat down on the bedspread, a compromise black-and-white pattern. It was the first time Lily had been in Tessa's room since the first day she had arrived, and looking around at it now, Lily caught her breath.

The horse poster Tessa's teacher had given her was hanging over the dresser, just the way Lily's horse poster was. There were drawings of horses on all the walls, the way Lily had done in her room — only these looked so much more artistic to Lily. Tessa's little motel bottles were arranged on a plate on her dresser — also shades of Lily — and the arrangement of art supplies on her desk was identical to Lily's.

The only thing different from Lily's room was the little photo taped just above the pillows. Only now, Lily saw, there were two photos. She crawled across the bed to get a closer look.

The one Tessa had put up the first day was of a pretty, dark-haired teenager holding a baby. The teenager was wearing a hospital gown, so it was obvious the baby was hers. And from the way the girl's green eyes looked proudly up at the camera, Lily knew she must be Tessa's mother.

The other photograph, right beside it, was Lily's school picture.

"That's me!" Lily said out loud. "She put me up there with her mom!"

Lily could feel her chest getting heavier. *And now she thinks I don't want her to be with me at the stables,* she thought. *Now she thinks I hate her or something.*

Lily let herself fall back on the bed. As she did, her head came down on something harder than the bedspread. It was Tessa's ragged binder, opened to a pencil drawing.

Lily rolled over on her stomach to look at it. It was a picture of two girls on a horse. Tessa wasn't skilled at drawing people yet, but the wild curly hair on the bigger girl was a dead giveaway. It was the two of them on Big Jake. Lily put her hand over her mouth. Engraved into the picture was a big X across Lily's chest.

Lily leaped from the bed and tore out of Tessa's room screaming her name. Mom met her halfway down the stairs.

"Lil, what on earth? What's going on?"

"I have to find Tessa!" Lily said. "She's gone! I have to find her and tell her I don't hate her!"

She dodged past Mom and took the rest of the stairs two at a time, still calling out Tessa's name.

"She's not down here," Joe said from the dining room table where he was calmly doing his homework. He rolled his eyes to the ceiling. "Thank you."

Lily ran into the family room anyway—and the kitchen—and Dad's study—the living room—the laundry room. She was nowhere.

Mom's face hardened as she checked the backyard and the garage. She told Joe to check the van, but Lily went with him. They all came back to the dining room without Tessa.

Mom turned into the marshal then. She had Joe check out the neighborhood on his bike and asked Lily to go into Dad's study and use his phone line to call the Girlz to see if she'd gone to any of them, while she used the house line to check out other possibilities.

After an hour — about the time Dad got home — they both shifted into an even more serious gear. Dad called the police.

"She didn't run away!" Lily said. "She wouldn't have gone without her picture of her mother and her binder. I *know* that!"

"We have to cover all the bases," Dad told her.

When Art got home, he tossed his backpack down and said, "I'm gonna go out and drive around and look for her."

"I'm going with you," Lily said.

She was almost out the door when Joe burst in from the garage. "That bike's missing!" he said. "That bike you got her — it's gone!"

"Let's go," Lily said to Art. Her thoughts were screaming at her.

Lily waited until they got in the car to tell Art: "I bet she rode her bike out to the Double H."

"All the way to Columbus! No way."

Then he and Lily looked at each other.

"Way," they said together.

It seemed to take forever to get there. Lily hung her head out the side window the whole way, scouring the side of the road with her eyes.

"She had a couple hours head start on us," Art said. "If that's where she was going, she's there by now."

Lily was out of the car before it had come to a full stop at the stables. And she was pouring out the story to Herbie almost before she got to him. He listened, his grim face telling her he hadn't seen her.

"So could I take Big Jake and go out and look for her in the field?" she said.

Herbie shook his head. "You can't ride Big Jake, Lily-girl. He's gone. I was just about to go look for him."

"Gone?" Lily said. "Did he run away—what happened?"

"I was up at the house having dinner. The horses were in for the night—"

"Could Tessa have taken him? Can she actually ride him?" Art said.

"He wasn't saddled up—"

"Hey, boss," Georgie called from the stable door. "You know anything about this? I found it in the hay."

He was holding a bike.

"That's Tessa's!" Lily said.

Herbie winced. "All right," he said. "Let's go."

Art went into the stable office to call Mom. Lily mounted Jiminy with Herbie, and they trotted off across the field. Lily held onto her chest to keep the tide that was building up in there from bursting loose. As they headed toward the creek, she whispered, "Please God—please God—" over and over.

The sun was setting, a bright orange over the silhouette of trees that would soon be completely dark.

"Should I be calling her name?" Lily said.

But Herbie didn't answer, and his body stiffened behind her.

"Over there," he said, pointing toward the stand of trees near the creek.

He gave Jiminy a sharp kick in the sides, and Lily held on as they took off at a gallop. Every fall of the hooves jarred painfully in her terrified chest.

Herbie reined Jiminy in and was off the horse—all in one swift motion. Lily scrambled down after him and looped the reins around a trunk before she took off to catch up. She nearly tripped over him, crouched at the edge of the creek.

Lily put her hand over her mouth to keep from screaming. Big Jake was there, lying down, eyes bulging and wild, whinnying from his throat.

Lily went down on her knees next to Herbie and stroked Big Jake's mane with her fingers. Even in the gathering darkness, she could see them shaking.

"You talk to him," Herbie said. "I'm going to check his legs."

Lily put her lips close to the horse's ear. "It's gonna be all right, boy," she said softly. "You just took a spill, but we'll have you up in a minute. It's gonna be all right."

She kept on, crooning, though she didn't believe a word she herself was saying.

"Got one broken," Herbie said. He ran his palm across his mouth and onto the back of his neck as he stared at the ground.

"Is it true about horses with broken legs?" Lily said. "Do you have to shoot them?"

Herbie didn't answer. Instead, he said, "Okay, we need help for old Jake here, and we have to find Tessa. I want you to take Jiminy back to the stables and call the vet. The number is right by the phone, on the wall."

Lily didn't argue, although she wanted more than anything to stay there with Jake—more than anything except finding Tessa. If Big Jake had gone down that hard—what had happened to *her?*

The ride back to the stables was like a dark dream. They were there before Lily even connected to the fact that she was on Herbie's horse. Jiminy seemed to know right where they were going—and why they needed to get there fast.

With trembling hands, Lily dialed the number on the wall. When she'd made the vet understand—in no uncertain terms—that this was a dire emergency and had described in minute detail exactly where Big Jake was, she banged the phone down and went toward Jiminy. But her knees buckled under her, and she stumbled into a bale of hay.

"Man, what's going on?" someone said behind her.

It was Art, and not two steps away, Dad. Lily stood up and fell into him, spilling out the story in a breathless voice.

"Where are they?" Dad said.

"I can take you," Lily said.

If it had been any other time, it would have been hilarious, getting Dad onto Jiminy behind her and ordering him to put his arms around her waist and hold on. When they arrived, Big Jake had his eyes closed, and he was breathing hard, as if he were afraid he would run out of air.

"Herbie?" Lily said.

Herbie emerged from the brush at the edge of the creek, just down from where Big Jake lay.

"Over here," he said. Even in the dark, his face looked to Lily to be even darker.

She and Dad followed him back into a thicket of just-blossoming wild iris. When Lily saw Tessa lying on the ground with Herbie's jacket covering her, she buckled again, and this time she went all the way to the dirt. From there she crawled to the tiny figure who, except for her short cap of dark hair, barely resembled the Tessa who could take a person down with one well-chosen nickname. In the stream of Herbie's flashlight, her face was so pale it looked almost transparent.

Dad, who was now on his knees beside her, put his fingers on the side of her throat and pressed.

"She has a pulse," Herbie said. "And she's breathing, but it's shallow."

*She's breathing?* Lily thought wildly. *Of course she's breathing! What are you talking about?*

"Go call 9-1-1, Lily," Dad said.

"You can take her back to the stables on Jiminy," Lily said. "I can walk —"

"We can't move her," Dad said sharply. "Now go —"

Lily was gone, and all she could do was hang on to Jiminy and cry all the way back to the stables.

She didn't stop crying until they were in the emergency room, where she and Art and Joe sat huddled together like a litter of puppies on the plastic chairs when Mom came out. Their tears and sobs froze on their faces. Mom was nearly as white as Tessa had been, and she was rubbing her fingers back and forth across her lips, over and over.

"What's the deal?" Art said.

"Come on, Mom," Joe said. "Dish." For someone who pretty much despised Tessa, Lily thought his voice was very shaky.

So Mom talked — and it was more than any of them could take in. Tessa had a concussion and a serious neck injury.

"Does that mean she's going to be paralyzed?" Art said.

"You mean, like a vegetable?" Joe said.

Lily just waited — waited for her mom to shake her head. But she didn't.

Chapter 15

"We just don't know the extent of her injuries," Mom said. "They won't know until after they operate."

"Operate?" Lily said.

"I've been operated on," Joe said. "It's not that bad, right?"

"It could be," Mom said. "It's going to be hours before she's out of surgery and conscious. I want you three to go home—"

"No," they all said in unison.

Mom looked way too tired to argue with them. She gave them all hugs and went back through the green curtains to Tessa.

"Tessa's not going to die, is she?" Lily asked.

Nobody answered until Joe said, "You know what's weird? I was always wishing that chick would drop off the face of the earth. But now I don't really want that. She was kinda startin' to change. I mean, she hasn't called me Loser in, like, three days."

"Yeah," Art said.

Lily was sure she could hear tears in his voice.

They all tried to stay awake, just in case news came down. Art even bought them coffee, though nobody but him could even get past the smell. One by one, they conked out, stretched across the chairs. Lily's feet were in Joe's hair, and her head was propped on Art's calves.

Gray light was creeping between the slats of the blinds when Lily woke up to the sound of Dad scraping a chair up close to theirs. She bolted straight up, nearly knocking Joe to the floor. He recurled himself and went back to sleep as Lily and Art rubbed their eyes.

"The operation went well," Dad said. "It was worse than they thought when they got in there, but they've repaired the damage. She's conscious now."

"And?" Art said.

"She can't move her legs yet," Dad said, looking at his own. "But they tell us it takes time and not to come to any drastic conclusions yet."

Lily began to shake her head. "This is all my fault," she said. "If I had made you guys let me take her to the stables, this wouldn't have happened."

"Like any of us ever made Mom and Dad do anything," Art said.

"It isn't your fault, Lilliputian," Dad said. "The way Tessa responds to things is a result of the way she's had to grow up. We've had her for a month. There is only so much healing you can do in a month."

Lily stood up, legs stiff, back like a pretzel. "I want to see her."

"I think that might cheer her up," Dad said. He gave her a dry smile. "She isn't liking any of this."

Lily's eyes were so swollen from crying she could barely see as she and Art followed Dad to the elevator and up to the second floor. Two burly men in outfits that matched the curtains were pushing Tessa down the hall from recovery to her room. Lily let go of Dad's hand and ran to her, walking beside her at a fast trot as the two men continued to roll her along.

"Tessa?" Lily said.

The green eyes opened, looking bigger than ever on her ghostly-white face. She couldn't move her head because of the large contraption that was holding her perfectly still. It looked scary, but Lily forged on.

"Tessa, I am *so* sorry this happened," she said. "I should have talked them into letting you come with me. I love you and—"

"Go away."

Lily stared.

Tessa's eyes closed again. "Make her go away," she said.

"You don't understand!" Lily cried. But she could feel someone's hands on her, pulling her back and leading her—somewhere. She didn't know where—and she didn't care. All she could do was cry out, "No! Let me explain it to her!"

But no one would. All the blurry people seemed intent on making her stop crying—on making her sleep. All she could think, as her eyes grew foggy, was that maybe God really had given up after all.

When Lily woke up, she was propped up against pillows on a couch in a dimly lit room with blankets tucked around her. A lady was sitting in a chair beside her with something in her hand that smelled good. When she talked, she sounded strangely like Reni's mother.

Lily blinked the blurriness out of her eyes and saw a spoon coming toward her.

"Chicken noodle," the lady said.

It *was* Reni's mom. Lily's head still felt like a bowl of oatmeal as she said, "Where's Reni?"

"Out in the hall," she said. "With the rest of the Girlz and—"

"Why aren't they in school?"

"Because school's out for the day," Mrs. Johnson said, chuckling. "Can they come in?"

"After you eat this. Now come on, open up."

Lily's mind began to clear as Mrs. Johnson spooned chicken and noodles into her mouth. She felt warm and good and comfortable for a minute, until she remembered.

"Tessa hates me," she said. She shook her head at the spoon.

Mrs. Johnson dimpled at her, the way Reni always did. "All right — maybe you need people who *don't* hate you. Shall I let them in?"

Lily nodded glumly.

She opened the door then, and the Girlz all filed in, faces so sober they looked like they were going to be in a police line-up.

The room was so small they could barely crowd in, and it was only after they all found places to sit on the arms of chairs and in each other's laps that she realized Shad Shifferdecker was with them. Somehow it didn't surprise her.

"What's this room for, anyways?" Shad said, squinting as he looked around.

"It's where they take the family after somebody dies," Reni said.

"Only nobody died," Suzy said quickly. "I mean, at least not Tessa."

"But she still can't move," Zooey said.

Kresha poked her.

"'Course, now she can't kick the wall any more," Zooey said.

"They said it takes time," Reni said, glaring at Zooey.

Lily sank hard into the pillow. "The whole thing was my fault. Now she hates me, and there's nothing I can do about it."

"She does?" Zooey said. "That's awful! Does she hate me too?"

"She doesn't hate anybody."

They all turned to look at Shad. He was sitting on the floor oppo-site Lily, slouched against the wall so that his feet disappeared under the couch.

"She hates me," Lily said.

"Nah," Shad said.

"How would you know?" Reni said.

"Because me and her's a lot alike."

"Oh, for Pete's sake," Zooey said. "In the first place, you're a boy and she's a girl, so—"

"It's like this," Shad said. "Her mom was, like, fourteen or some-thing when she had the kid and she tried to take care of her and she couldn't, so she gave her to somebody else. That's the first thing—your own mom gives you up, ya feel like garbage or somethin'. So she trusts these people that take her, 'cause she's still young. But she starts actin' up a little, y'know, tryin' to let people know she's messed up about it, only nobody gets it because she's like, two years old. So then them people pass her on to somebody else 'cause they can't handle her and she feels, y'know—"

"Rejected," Reni said.

"Yeah—rejected. And it stinks."

Heads nodded. Kresha and Zooey looked ready to cry.

"So," Shad went on, "by this time she's, like, six, and she figures to keep from gettin' hurt again, she ain't gonna trust nobody no more. If somebody can like her even when she's what they call actin' out, then maybe she *might* trust 'em." Shad shrugged. "'Course, nobody ever did, so that whole thing kept goin', 'til—"

"'Til she came to us," Lily said. Her voice sounded stiff, even to her. "And that's why she was acting out even though we were doing all that nice stuff for her."

114

"How'd you know about acting out?" Reni said to Shad.

"'Cause I done it myself, and that's what my shrink called it."

"What's a shrink?" Zooey said.

"It doesn't matter now," Lily said. "We did everything, and look what happened."

"What happened?" Shad said.

"She gave up," Lily said. "She even gave up on me. It was like we were getting to be—and then this happened—and now—"

"And now if ya stop," Shad said, "she'll go right down the toilet like I was gonna do—only my aunt, well, my mom, she just kept raggin' on me and slobberin' on me and stuff—"

"Slobbering?" Zooey said.

"Look," Shad said. "She's, like, this close—" He held two fingers so that they almost touched.

"How you know?" Kresha said.

Shad didn't even hesitate. He spoke confidently, as if he were talking about his last trip to Burger King. "My mom and dad went to jail when I was, like, three," he said, "so the court gave me to my aunt, and she adopted me, and she was in my face all the time—like 24/7." He shrugged casually. "I just quit actin' out about six months ago."

"You *did*?" Zooey said.

"So what *do* we do?" Reni said. "It's obvious we gotta do something."

Lily felt tears coming as she looked at Reni—at all the Girlz. They were sitting up straight, looking at Shad with trust in their eyes, as if he *hadn't* been their chief tormentor since the fourth grade. And Reni was saying, "We gotta do something."

*They're not giving up*, she thought. *Maybe we can get Tessa back—even if God did give up.*

"Go for it, Shad," Reni said. "And Suzy—get a piece of paper and a pencil—you got one in your bag?"

Suzy nodded, and Reni lifted her chin toward Shad. "Let's get started. We've got planning to do."

Lily was sure she saw Shad's usually concave chest puff out a little. For the next thirty minutes, they bent their heads together, which wasn't hard to do in that small room, and sorted through ideas for Suzy to write down.

"Looks like a plan to me," Reni said, just as the door opened and Mom poked her head in.

"Oh, no, please, Girlz," she said. "No plans right now, okay?" She looked like her team had just lost the championship as she picked her way through the bodies to sit on the edge of the couch where Lily was. Her shoulders sagged forward.

Lily felt fear licking at her insides. "Mom?" she said. "Is she—"

"The same," Mom said. "And, guys, as much as I love your faith and your hope, no Girlz Only plan is going to change that, I don't think. Just pray, okay?"

Lily drooped, but the Girlz sat up straighter. "This plan *is* like a prayer," Reni said. "I think you're gonna love it."

And when they told her about it, she did.

Mom had only one suggestion about the plan. She said that Tessa was still groggy from all the pain medication they were giving her, and the Girlz needed to give her a few days to get to the place where she really knew who was there and what they were saying.

"She thought I was the Stay-Puff Marshmallow Man," Mom said. Her lips twitched for the first time in hours. "I think she's seen *Ghostbusters* a few too many times."

Lily started to deflate, but Reni quickly said, "This'll just give us more time to get ready."

"Come," Kresha said. "We go ask Art to be our shuffler."

"Shuffler?" Mom said.

"She means chauffeur," Suzy said.

"Ah," Mom said. She turned to Lily, who was finally freeing herself from the couch. "That will be good for Art. If he paces the hall much longer, he's going to wear a path in it."

For the next two days, the Girlz, Shad, and Art prepared for the plan. Even Joe got into the act.

"I know what it's like lyin' there not bein' able to do sports," Joe said. "When she gets home, I'll give her my turns with the remote."

"Somebody write that down," Art said.

On Saturday Zooey and Kresha did their part, though all of the Girlz and Shad went to the hospital to wait in the hall outside Tessa's room. Reni said they should pray first, and they made a circle holding hands, with Shad shuffling around in the background. Lily wanted to shuffle with him, but she closed her eyes and was quiet as Reni led off.

Zooey let out a huge breath when they were done. "I'm not scared now," she said. "I was before—I mean, what if she hated me too, like she does Lily?"

"Heeey, Zooey," Art said. "Forget a career as a diplomat, okay?"

*I guess Zooey hasn't given up on God,* Lily thought. But she couldn't make herself feel the same way. It was all up to them now.

Zooey and Kresha gave Tessa her last spelling test, which she had taken just before the accident and which the teacher had put a big B+ on. Zooey and Kresha had put it in a frame decorated with stars and Good Job! stickers. They also left Tessa's schoolbooks there in a stack, tied with ribbon. Then Kresha told Tessa exactly what the Girlz had told her to say. "When you're feeling up to it, we're going to be here to help you get caught up in school. We aren't giving up on you."

Zooey and Kresha waited until Tessa went back to sleep and then sat by the bed and prayed for her. It had started the Robbinses' whole church praying for her when Mom told the pastor about the Girlz' plan. He promised there would be people praying around the clock.

*If I were going to pray,* Lily wrote in her journal that night, *if I hadn't given up on you fixing this for me, I would pray that Tessa would be able to walk again, and that she wouldn't hate me, and that Herbie wouldn't hate me either because of what happened to Big Jake, and that Jake would still be alive.*

"If I were going to pray," Lily said to Otto.

Even with him there and China back, it felt lonely.

"Okay, so maybe I'll pray just a little," she told them. "At least Tessa didn't tell Zooey and Kresha to go away." She picked up her pen again and wrote, *God — if you haven't given up — then maybe I won't. Just — help us, okay?*

But even after that, Lily was still so restless she could barely sit down. She found it almost impossible to do her schoolwork and couldn't stay at the table long enough to eat a whole meal. Even Otto seemed calm in comparison.

On Sunday it was Reni's and Suzy's turn to visit Tessa after church and give her the big certificate that said FINEST FRISBEE FIEND and a brand-new Frisbee. Art dropped them off at the hospital, along with Zooey and Kresha, but he told Lily to stay in the car.

"I want to be there!" Lily said. "I'm going crazy enough as it is!"

"Mom and Dad want me to take you someplace else."

"Where?" Lily said.

"You'll see."

She saw as they headed toward Columbus. She didn't have to be a rocket scientist to know they were going to the Double H.

"If it's more bad news, Art, I can't take it," Lily said.

"Herbie said on the phone it wasn't bad."

"You talked to Herbie?"

"Mom did. He said he wants you to come out and see him."

"I'm scared," Lily said.

119

She could hear her voice quavering, and she felt small and raw as she watched Columbus come to her in a blur. Everyone was in on the plan together. Why did she suddenly feel so alone?

"What is it we're tellin' Tessa?" Art said. "Don't give up on God?"

"I wonder if anybody told Big Jake that," Lily said.

Herbie met Lily at the open stable doors, just like always, but to Lily the stables were a different place. They seemed darker inside, as if the sun no longer crept in from the other end. Lily was sure the horses were all turning their eyes away from her. But Herbie threw an arm around her shoulder and gave her a side squeeze.

"I hear the Little Girlie is coming along," he said.

"I think you heard wrong," Lily said. "She still can't move her legs."

"There's more than one way to make progress. Now take Big Jake."

Lily felt her heart skip. "Big Jake?" she said. "He's still — alive?"

"He's here, and he's been asking for you," Herbie said. "I told him you had the Little Girlie to look after, but he kept nagging."

Herbie was leading the way into another part of the stables, where there was a stall Lily had never seen anyone use before. Lily followed, trying not to breathe in the smells that had always made her feel at home. Now they made her feel *homesick*.

"This is the infirmary," Herbie said, chuckling. "But not for long. Big Jake — he doesn't give up."

The words startled Lily — and so did the sight of Big Jake. The big horse was in a giant sling that hung from the ceiling. It cradled his belly and let his legs dangle above the ground. One of them was in another contraption that made Tessa's neck apparatus look like a toy.

"He *is* still alive!" Lily said.

"You bet he is, Lily-girl. And if you don't start petting him, he's going to crash right out of there."

Lily tiptoed toward Big Jake and put a shaky hand up to stroke his cheek. He pushed his nose into her palm and sniffed. His soft breath was like a prayer as she put her forehead on his muzzle.

"You're okay," she said. "I thought it was my fault that you broke your leg and had to be shot—but you're okay!"

"Jake's been with me too long for me to put him down," Herbie said. "It was a nice clean break, anyway."

"Will anybody ever ride him again?" Lily said as she stroked Jake's mane with one hand and swatted at her tears with the other.

"Not so much," Herbie said. "But you're going to have to come out here and keep him company 'til he gets adjusted to that. You and Tessa both—and she's going to need to get back on a horse as soon as she can. She can ride with you at first if she wants."

Lily shook her head. "I don't think Tessa's going to want to ride with me—even if she does get better. She hates me now."

Herbie tipped his hat back with his finger and looked at her closely. "What makes you think a thing like that?" he said. "That girl thinks you're the best thing since sliced bread."

Lily shook her head and told him what was happening at the hospital with Tessa, including the Girlz' plan and Shad's part in it.

"He and I are supposed to go tomorrow," she told Herbie, "and I want to see her so bad—but I'm scared she's going to hate me forever."

Herbie was quiet as he took off his hat and rubbed the bandana on his head. "We can't have that, Lily-girl," he said. "We just can't have that."

When it was time for Lily to leave school for the hospital the next day, she felt shaky in the knees, probably from being so nervous she hadn't been able to eat lunch.

To her surprise, it was Mom who picked her up, not Art.

"What's wrong, Mom?" Lily said as she leaped into the van. "Is she worse?"

"No," Mom said calmly. "I just wanted a few minutes with you."

"Did she tell you she didn't want to see me?"

"I haven't asked her," Mom said. "I'm letting this be a surprise, just the way you all planned it. But, Lil, please remember that she's absolutely terrified that she'll never walk again. I know she's eaten up with guilt about it too. And Tessa turns feeling guilty into blaming someone else."

"So she's blaming me."

"Maybe. But what really concerns me is that you're going in there terrified too. She shouldn't see that. She should see the old Lily who never gives up. The one who believes that God doesn't give up."

Lily stared at her lap. "I don't know if I really believe that anymore, Mom."

"I know," Mom said. "I've watched you these past couple of days."

Lily looked at her. Mom's face was smooth.

"You aren't going to tell me I'm wrong?"

"Don't have to. You're going to find that out yourself. And I know you will, because other people haven't given up. Other people have been praying. And besides all that," Mom gave her a sideways glance, "God doesn't give up. You can't possibly think that when you look at how Tessa did *not* die from a very serious neck injury — and how Herbie chose *not* to put Big Jake down even though that sling contraption is costing him a bundle — and how Shad Shifferdecker has practically become a permanent fixture in this whole thing. Not to mention someone else who has entered the picture —"

Lily looked at Mom again. Her mouth was twitching.

"Who?" Lily said.

"You'll see," Mom said. "You'll see that God has definitely not given up. Now don't *you* give up on *him*."

*But what if it's too late?* Lily thought as she rode the elevator up to Tessa's floor with Mom. *What if God's mad at me now for giving up?* She squeezed her eyes shut and prayed. *Please don't be mad at me—I'm just so scared.*

Shad was waiting for her outside the door, the T-shirts he'd brought stuffed in a wad under his arm.

And just as Mom had said, there was someone else there too. It was Herbie, wearing his battered hat and a gap-toothed smile.

"How you doing, Lily-girl?" he said, giving her the side squeeze.

"I'm—what are you doing here?"

"Came to see if you could use my help," Herbie said. He winked. "Big Jake sent me. He told me to bring this." He held up a shopping bag.

"Oh, no!" Lily said. "I left my gift in Art's car."

"And Art—being the amazing individual that he is—brought it here for you," said Art, as he strode down the hall lugging China.

"Just wait out here with him until I tell you," Lily said.

"I know the drill," Art said. He looked at Mom. "I see you didn't have much luck calming her down."

"Where are the Girlz? I want to pray before we go in—"

"They're getting a snack down at the vending machines," Art said.

Shad grunted. "So what?" he said. "We can't pray without them?"

Mom's mouth twitched as she put out her hands for holding. "Absolutely we can," she said. "The Lord be with you."

So they prayed, Herbie's hand in Lily's right, Shad's in her left. Shad's palm was clammy—so Lily knew he was as nervous as she was. Herbie's was callused and strong. It felt wise.

Lily clung to both of them, and she prayed—for real. When she looked up, Mom was smiling at her.

"Don't give up on God, Lil," she whispered as Shad pushed open the door to Tessa's room.

Lily took one more deep prayer breath and followed him in. Still, although Shad and Herbie went straight to the head of the bed, Lily stayed at the foot, clutching China against her.

"Hey, girlfriend," Shad said to Tessa.

"What are you doing here?" Tessa said.

It was the first time Lily had heard her voice in almost a week. It sounded husky and pulled-back. *What happened to the real Tessa?* Lily thought. *Is she still in there?*

"Brought ya a present," Shad said. He held up one of the T-shirts so she could see the words: ROBBINS ROWDIES — Championship Frisbee Team.

Tessa was quiet as Shad showed her the names on the back. When Shad said, "Cool, huh?" she said, "Like, I'm ever gonna get to wear one."

Lily felt herself sagging against the end of the bed, but she forced herself to stand up straight. *I won't give up on you, God,* she said in her head. *I won't give up.*

Shad looked a little saggy himself as he jammed the T-shirts back under his arm and stuck his hands in his pockets. Lily had never seen him look helpless before.

Herbie leaned over Tessa and grinned into her face. "You remember me, don't you, Little Girlie?"

Lily was sure she heard a gasp come out of Tessa.

"Did you come here to yell at me?" she said. "'Cause if you did—"

"Don't get all in an uproar," Herbie said. "I came to give you this." He pulled a white cowboy hat out of the shopping bag and hung it on the IV bottle that swung above her. "This is what you'll wear when you come out and get back on a horse."

"I'm never riding a horse again," Tessa said. The words came out like pieces of wood.

"Oh, yes, you are," Herbie said. "Now you listen to me."

He leaned in so that Tessa had to look at him. The device that held her head in place was turning out to be a handy little thing.

"Things went bad with Big Jake," he said. "And that was because of mistakes you made. But you won't make those mistakes again because you learned."

"So?" Tessa said. "It's too late now."

She was speaking so low now, Lily had to lean in to hear her, pressing her hands on the end of the bed.

"It's never too late," Herbie said. "When you fall off a horse, it's never too late to get back on and try again." He touched her arm. "It's the same with people. You keep trying with them. And I hear you're doing that."

"I can't do anything lying in this stupid bed."

"You promised the other girlies you'd let them help you with your schoolwork—lying right here in this bed. And you listened when they told you that you'd play Frisbee again, right from where you are right now. That's trying."

Tessa didn't answer. Herbie leaned closer—so close that his nose was just inches from hers.

"So what I want to know," he said, "is why you won't try with Lily."

Lily's hands tightened on the bed.

"Is she here?" Tessa said, voice rising. "Is that her down there?"

Herbie nodded at Lily. She sucked in air.

"It's me," she said. "I brought you a present too."

She swallowed hard. Herbie hoisted China up—with Shad's help—and displayed his newly repaired tummy for Tessa. His scar was covered with a heart that said "I'm yours."

Tessa closed her eyes. "Go away," she said.

"Don't do that, Tessa!" Lily said. "Please don't!"

Herbie put his finger to his lips as he looked at Lily, and then he leaned into Tessa again.

"You're thinking, what if trusting doesn't work, like so many times before?" Herbie said. "That's it, isn't it?"

"Yeah," Shad said.

Lily looked up at him quickly. He looked as if Herbie were talking to him instead of Tessa.

"That's it, isn't it, Little Girlie?" Herbie said. "You can afford to try and fail with the other girls and even Shad here. But not with Lily. She matters more, doesn't she?"

Lily watched Tessa, praying that her eyes would open and she would look at her. But Tessa's face crumpled, and she let out a cry — like a toddler in a store who'd lost her mom.

"She matters more than anybody," Tessa said.

"But I'm right here!" Lily said. "And I'm not gonna give up on you — and God's not gonna give up on you."

It was all she could say. It was hard to talk with a breaking heart.

The door came open just then, and a nurse bustled in.

"What's going on?" she said. "Do you need more pain medication?"

"Go away," Tessa said. Her streaming eyes searched the ceiling. "I just want Lily."

Herbie gave Lily a misty-eyed smile and followed the nurse out of the room. Lily stretched to get her face closer to Tessa's.

"You're supposed to sleep now, and we're supposed to pray," she said.

"You won't leave?" Tessa said.

"No way," Lily said.

"I won't let her," Shad said.

Tessa took a few minutes to drop off to sleep. When she did, Shad slunk over and sat in the chair next to Lily beside the bed.

"It's creepy with all them tubes and needles and stuff," he whispered. "I'd be rippin' those out."

"No, you would not, either," Lily whispered back. "You talk all big, but I saw you just now when Herbie was talking."

"You tell anybody, and I'll—"

"Don't worry. The Girlz and I—we don't give away each other's secrets."

Shad grinned. "So I'm one of the Girlz now?"

"Hey—you guys," Tessa said.

"You're supposed to be asleep," Lily said.

"Yeah—but I wanna show you guys something. Look at this."

"Look at what?" Lily said.

"Her feet!" Shad said. "Look at 'em—they're movin'!"

Lily stared as the two bumps in the sheets shifted, ever so little, from side to side.

"Are you doing that, Tessa?" Lily said.

"Yes! Look—I'm doin' it!"

"She's doin' it!" Shad cried.

And then he looked at Lily and scooped her into a hug. They, of course, pulled away after about a half a second and split off to either side of the bed as if they were dodging bullets. But Lily didn't have the urge to shake off cooties. She leaned into Tessa's face and saw a tear sliding out of the corner of her eye.

"Thanks for not givin' up on me," Tessa said.

"I never will," she said. "And God's not giving up on you either." She kissed Tessa on the forehead. "After all," she said, "you're my sister."

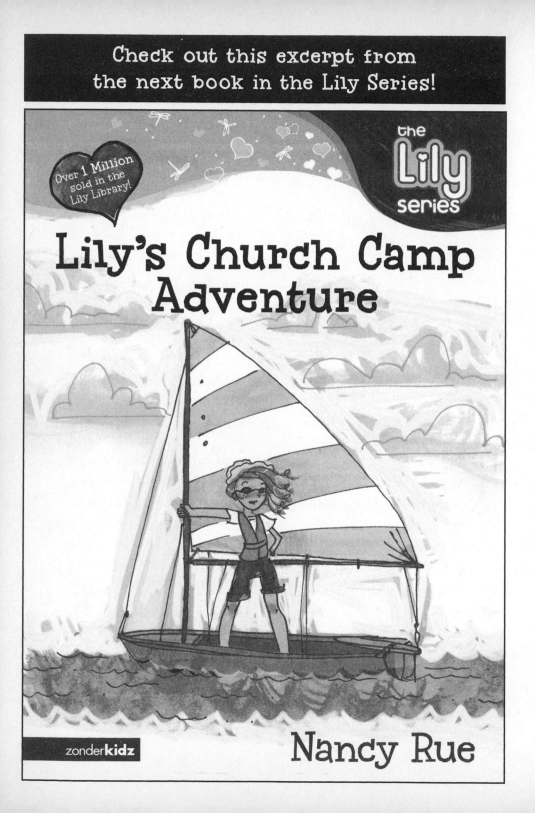

# Lily's Church Camp Adventure

## Nancy Rue

**Chapter 1**

"I still say it's not fair."

Lily Robbins looked up from her suitcase at her younger sister, Tessa, who was letting both arms flop to the bed, over and over and over—and, oh yes, over. Lily knew Tessa would have been doing it with her legs if the body brace she was wearing had let her. It was what she did when she was afraid and wouldn't admit it.

"What are you scared of?" Lily said as she tried to cram one more Camp Galilee T-shirt into her already stuffed duffel bag.

"I'm not scared of nothin'," Tessa said, scowling. "I just said it ain't fair."

"Isn't fair."

"That's what I said!" The arms did a particularly hard flop. "It's not fair that I gotta stay here while you go to some dumb camp for two weeks."

Lily felt her lips twitch. "If it's dumb, why would you want to go anyway?"

Tessa's scowl deepened until Lily was sure her forehead was going to meet her chin. Nobody could scowl like Tessa.

"Besides," Lily said, "you're just now getting back on your feet since the accident. You'd have to sit and watch everybody else hike and rock climb and sail—" She stopped. Tessa's eyes were going into slits.

"Are you scared of being here without me?" Lily said.

"No, that's dumb."

"Are you scared you'll miss me so much you'll cry?"

"That's double dumb!"

Lily climbed on top of her duffel bag and squished it down while she pulled the zipper closed. The bulging sides puckered, and she could almost hear her clothes groaning. She swiveled to face Tessa, who was still trying to maintain the scowl. Lily could see her big green eyes misting up.

"Are you scared I'm not coming back or something?"

"No!" Tessa said. She slammed her arms down so hard that China, Lily's big stuffed panda, bounced two inches off the bed. Tessa turned her glare on him, so that all Lily could see was the wavy back of Tessa's short dark hair. "You're gonna forget about me while you're gone," she said. "That's what's gonna happen."

"No way!" Lily said. She scrambled up and sat next to Tessa on the bed. Otto, Lily's mutt dog, took that as his cue to join them and crawled out from under the bed and hopped up. Lily stroked his head and Tessa's at the same time. "I'm only gonna be gone two weeks," she said. "But even if I was gone the whole summer—or a whole year even—I wouldn't forget you. You're my sister."

"Adopted," Tessa muttered. "And I ain't even that yet. That dumb judge still has to make it—what's that word?"

"Official," Lily said. "But I don't need him to do that. You're my sister already, and I'm not gonna forget you, so quit talking like a freak."

Tessa turned to Lily and scoured her face with her eyes as if she were digging for traces of a lie. "Do you wish I was goin'?" she said.

"Well, yeah, du-uh!" Lily said. And she did. Tessa was still pretty rowdy and definitely stubborn, but she was nothing like the way she was when she'd first come to live with the Robbins family. Lily was having trouble imagining what it was going to be like not having Tessa tagging after her every minute, asking ten thousand questions. Tessa was what Dad called streetwise, but she didn't know a lot of stuff most nine-year-olds knew. Lily had taken it upon herself to teach her.

*If I weren't so jazzed about this camp,* Lily thought, *I'd stay home and help Mom and Dad work with her.* But her parents had urged her to go. They said they needed some one-on-one time with Tessa anyway — and Camp Galilee was the best Christian camp for girls in the whole eastern United States — or so everybody said. Mom and Dad were sure that if anybody would enjoy the special programs they had at Galilee, it was Lily.

Besides, the Girlz were all going — Reni and Suzy and Zooey and even Kresha. Their church had made sure Kresha got a scholarship since her mom didn't have a lot of money.

*I have to spend all the time I can with my Girlz this summer,* Lily thought. *The end of August is gonna be here before I know it, and then I won't see them for a whole year. A whole year!*

"You wanna go real bad," Tessa said. She was still studying Lily's face.

"Yeah, I do," Lily said. She had to be honest with Tessa. The kid had lie radar. "But I also wanna be with you. Too bad I can't be in two places at one time."

Otto gave a growl and wriggled away from Lily, squirming as close to Tessa's side as he could, and sighed himself in. So far, Tessa was the only other person in the Robbins family besides Lily that Otto would even allow to touch him. Ever since she had come home from the hospital, he had to be on the couch or the bed or the chair next to Tessa. The only exception was at night, when, as always, he crawled under Lily's covers like a mole and slept there.

"Look at him," Lily said. "I bet by the time I get back, he'll have forgotten about me and only want you."

"Not gonna happen," Tessa said—although the scowl did fade a little at the prospect. "I'll make sure he doesn't forget you." Her eyes suddenly took on an impish gleam. "And I'll make sure Shad Shifferdecker doesn't forget about you either."

Lily felt her blue eyes narrowing. "That's really okay," she said.

"You know he likes you," Tessa said.

Lily grunted and got up to go to the dresser, where she raked a brush through her mane of red curly hair. She could see her usually pale face going blotchy in the mirror.

"You like him too—you know you do," Tessa said.

"Shut up!" Lily said.

In the mirror, she could see Tessa grinning.

There was a knock on the door, and Art, Lily's seventeen-year-old brother, poked his head in. "Dad wants to know if your bag is ready yet," he said. "He's got the air conditioner going in the van, and he's ready to roll."

Lily nodded toward her duffel bag and finished the second pigtail she'd just tamed her hair into. She grabbed the khaki hat that matched her shorts and perched it on top of her head. She gazed at her Camp Galilee T-shirt in the mirror. She was a camper from head to toe.

"Good grief—what have you got in here?" Art said. His face went red as he hoisted Lily's bag up onto his shoulder.

"My stuff," Lily said.

"You're going to camp, for Pete's sake," Art said, grunting his way to the door. "All you need's two pairs of shorts and a couple of T-shirts."

"And underwear and socks."

"Nobody changes underwear and socks at camp."

"Gross me out and make me icky!" Lily said. "Just go—oh, wait—I forgot something."

"How could you have forgotten something? Everything you own has to be in this bag."

"Stop! I gotta put my journal in there!"

Lily stuck her hand between her mattresses and pulled out her talking-to-God journal and its special purple gel pen.

"Put it in your backpack," Art said as he maneuvered his way out the door. "I'm not picking this thing up again. I'm about to get a hernia as it is."

"What's a hernia?" Tessa said.

"Don't try to come downstairs by yourself, Squirt," Art said to her over his shoulder. "I'll come back and get you for the big tear fest."

"What tear fest?" Lily said, following him down the steps.

"You're leaving for two weeks," Art said. "You're going to cry."

"I am not. Why would I cry?"

"You cry over commercials for AT&T long distance," Art said. "Of course you're gonna cry."

Lily ignored him and jockeyed impatiently from side to side as Art made his way to the first floor and out the front door. Mom was waiting there, and Lily's ten-year-old brother, Joe, was on his knees on a chair behind her, batting at her ponytail like a cat.

"Can I have Lily's share of dessert while she's gone?" he said.

"Sure," Mom said, brown eyes dancing. "And you can also have her share of chores." Her mouth twitched in that way it did instead of outright smiling. Suddenly Lily felt a pang. She wasn't going to see her mom twitch her lips for two whole weeks. She'd never been away from her for longer than a weekend.

"I'm gonna go up and get the squirt," Art said as he charged through the door and headed for the stairs. Although it was barely light out, his T-shirt was sticking to his back with sweat.

"Too late," Joe said.

Tessa was almost to the bottom of the steps. *One more reason why she can't go to camp,* Lily thought. *She still doesn't do what you tell her to do half the time.*

133

But another shivery pang went through Lily. She was going to miss that too—and Otto—and the horse Big Jake out at the ranch nuzzling her neck with his soft nose. She was even going to miss Joe, the absurd little creep. The wonderful absurd little creep.

"Let's go, Lilliputian," Dad said from the doorway. He was wearing a moustache of perspiration, and even his graying red hair was sparkling with sweat. "I wish I were going to Maine to sit by the bay for two weeks."

*And I wish I wasn't! Not without all of you guys!*

Lily didn't know where the thought came from, but as Mom hugged her and told her to have an amazing time and not to try to run the place the first day, Lily felt herself fighting back tears. She struggled to keep it from turning into a tear fest only because she didn't want Art to be right. Sniffing while Dad pulled out of the driveway and onto the street, she waved until Tessa was merely a dot on the front porch.

But the minute Kresha bounded out of her apartment building— clothes poking out of her duffel bag, sand-colored hair sticking out of a lopsided ponytail, and a grin spreading ear to ear—Lily's urge to cry disappeared.

"We are going to the camp, Lee-Lee!" Kresha cried. Lily grabbed her hands and jumped up and down with her while Dad shoved Kresha's bag into the van. *I hope no one makes fun of her Croatian accent at camp,* Lily thought before reassuring herself. *Nah—we'll always be there to protect her.*

They both climbed happily into the van, and the happiness built as they picked up each of the Girlz and headed north on the New Jersey Turnpike. They passed around a bag of Doritos to each other—since everyone had been too excited to eat breakfast—and switched seats a half dozen times. And, of course, their mouths ran nonstop.

"Okay—how *cool* is this gonna be, guys?" Reni said.

"You're not scared there won't be any other African-American girls there?" Zooey said. Her brow furrowed under her carefully curled bangs. Zooey was their worrier.

Reni raised an eyebrow at her. "Not that I was even thinking about it," she said, "but my mom checked into it, and there's ten of us."

"Besides," Lily said, "it's not gonna matter because we're all gonna be in the same cabin." She darted her eyes from girl to girl. "You guys did request each other on the form, right?"

"You asked us that eight thousand times," Zooey said.

"And I checked them all when we filled them out," Suzy said, nodding her shiny bob of dark hair.

"Then it's a done deal," Reni said. Suzy, after all, was probably more efficient than the school secretary.

"What we do tonight in our *cabin*?" Kresha said. She'd been practicing saying that word for two weeks.

"Pillow fight," Reni said.

"Unless it's against the rules," Suzy said.

"Let's not tell scary stories," Zooey said. "I won't be able to sleep."

"I say we play a game," Lily said.

Reni grinned slyly. "What kind of game, Lil?"

"I don't know. I'll think of something."

"You do always, Lee-Lee," Kresha said.

Lily nestled back into the seat and smiled to herself. This was going to be the best. She and her Girlz would be together for two weeks with nothing to do but have fun and "discover a relationship with God." That was what the brochure had said. *I'm gonna be good at that,* Lily thought. *I already have one.* She didn't cuddle in with China and Otto and her talking-to-God journal every night for nothing.

"You know what I love?" Zooey said.

"What?" Lily said.

"We're not going to have to worry about Chelsea and Ashley and all of them the whole time we're gone."

Reni grunted. "I *don't* worry about them."

But Lily knew what Zooey meant. Chelsea and Ashley and their friends were the popular girls at Cedar Hills Middle School, and they never let the Girlz forget that *they* were never going to be "popular." Even though the Girlz had stopped buying into that and were finding their own happiness, Lily had to agree that it was going to be good not to have to deal with it.

"What about Shad?" Reni said.

Lily snapped her a look. "What about him?" she said.

"Are you glad to be away from him too?" Reni said, dimples going deep into her cheeks.

Lily felt red blotches forming on her neck, like they always did when she wanted to hide her head in a hole. There was a time when she would have answered that question with a loud, "Gross me out and make me icky!" But Shad wasn't so icky anymore, and that was pretty confusing.

"Lily!" Zooey said. "You *do* like him, don't you?"

Only because Lily saw her father's ears practically coming to a point did she not shove an entire Rice Krispies treat into Zooey's mouth. Instead, she said, "Give it up, Zo. I'm not going there."

The scenery changed as the day went on and they wound their way through New England. Trees arched over them, creating a welcome trellis, and Dad told them to roll down their windows so they could smell the air. It was cool on their arms and made Lily want to breathe until her whole chest filled up.

That afternoon they could smell salty air and watch seagulls circling as if they'd been waiting to guide them to Camp Galilee near the ocean. The further they drove, the more clearly Lily could imagine the five of them and their counselor setting out on Penobscot Bay in sailboats with bright striped sails.

"I *really* want to go sailing," she said to the Girlz.

"Doesn't everybody get to sail?" Reni said.

Suzy shook her head. "It says it right in the brochure. Every cabin has a different activity."

"Ours has to be sailing," Lily said. "I've read three books on it."

She didn't add that she hadn't understood most of it. It still sounded like the most exciting thing she could imagine—and she had imagined some pretty exhilarating things in her time.

"I hope we get a counselor that isn't mean," Zooey said.

"Didn't the brochure say all the counselors were college students?" Lily said.

"Yes," Suzy said. "Right on page two."

"Is that what it said?" Dad grinned. "I think I'd better take you home then."

Dad was a college professor. He was always moaning about university students and their shenanigans. Lily didn't care whether they had shenanigans or not—whatever that was. It was going to be cool.

Long after lunch, a sign appeared pointing its arrow down a winding road where they could already see Penobscot Bay. The Girlz all cheered and didn't stop until Dad brought the van to a halt in front of a building that had a big banner on it, which read:

## WELCOME TO CAMP GALILEE
## REGISTER HERE

"How ya doin'!" said a bubbly, short girl of about nineteen as she opened Lily's door. "Drop your bags over here, and get your cabin assignments over there!"

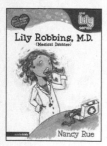
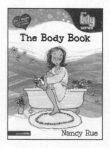

### Lily and the Creep (Book Three)

Softcover • ISBN-10: 0-310-23252-X
ISBN-13: 978-0-310-23252-0

Lily learns what it means to be a child of God
and how to develop God's image in herself.

### The Buddy Book

Softcover • ISBN-10: 0-310-70064-7
ISBN-13: 978-0-310-70064-7
(Companion Nonfiction to *Lily and the Creep*)

*The Buddy Book* is all about relationships—why they're important,
how lousy your life can be if they're crummy, what makes a good
one, and how God is the Counselor for all of them.

### Lily's Ultimate Party (Book Four)

Softcover • ISBN-10: 0-310-23253-8
ISBN-13: 978-0-310-23253-7

After Lily's plans for the "ultimate" party fall apart, her grandmother shows
Lily that having a party for the right reasons will help to make it a success.

### The Best Bash Book

Softcover • ISBN-10: 0-310-70065-5
ISBN-13: 978-0-310-70065-4
(Companion Nonfiction to *Lily's Ultimate Party*)

*The Best Bash Book* provides fun party ideas and alternatives,
as well as etiquette for hosting and attending parties.

### Ask Lily (Book Five)

Softcover • ISBN-10: 0-310-23254-6
ISBN-13: 978-0-310-23254-4

Lily becomes the "Answer Girl" and gives
anonymous advice in the school newspaper.

### The Blurry Rules Book

Softcover • ISBN-10: 0-310-70152-X
ISBN-13: 978-0-310-70152-1
(Companion Nonfiction to *Ask Lily*)

Explaining ethics for an 8-12 year old girl! You will discover that although there
may not always be an easy answer or a concrete rule, there's always a God answer.

*Available now at your local bookstore!*

**zonderkidz**

### Lily the Rebel (Book Six)

Softcover • ISBN-10: 0-310-23255-4
ISBN-13: 978-0-310-23255-1

Lily starts to question the rules at home and at school and decides she may not want to follow the rules.

### The It's MY Life Book

Softcover • ISBN-10: 0-310-70153-8
ISBN-13: 978-0-310-70153-8
(Companion Nonfiction to *Lily the Rebel*)
*The It's MY Life Book* is designed to help you find balance in your struggle for independence, so you can become not only your best self, but most of all your God-intended self.

### Lights, Action, Lily! (Book Seven)

Softcover • ISBN-10: 0-310-70249-6
ISBN-13: 978-0-310-70249-8

Cast in a Shakespearean play at school by a mere fluke, Lily is immediately convinced she's destined for a career on Broadway, but finally learns through a series of entanglements that relationships are more important than a perfect performance.

### The Creativity Book

Softcover • ISBN-10: 0-310-70247-X
ISBN-13: 978-0-310-70247-4
(Companion Nonfiction to *Lights, Action, Lily!*)
Discover your creativity and learn to enjoy the arts in this fun, activity-filled book written by Nancy Rue.

### Lily Rules! (Book Eight)

Softcover • ISBN-10: 0-310-70250-X
ISBN-13: 978-0-310-70250-4

Lily is voted class president at her school, but unlike her predecessors who have been content to sail along with the title and a picture in the yearbook, Lily is out to make changes.

### The Uniquely Me Book

Softcover • ISBN- 10: 0-310-70248-8
ISBN- 13: 978-0-310-70248-1
(Companion Nonfiction to *Lily Rules!*)
At some point, every girl wonders why she was born and why she's the way she is. Well, author Nancy Rue has written the perfect book designed to answer all those nagging uncertainties from a biblical perspective.

*Available now at your local bookstore!*

### zonderkidz

### Rough & Rugged Lily (Book Nine)

Softcover • ISBN-10: 0-310-70260-7
ISBN-13: 978-0-310-70260-3

Lily's convinced she's destined to become a great outdoorswoman, but when the Robbins family is stranded in a snowstorm on the way to a mountain cabin to celebrate Christmas, she learns the real meaning of survival and how dependent she is on the material things of life.

### The Year 'Round Holiday Book

Softcover • ISBN-10: 0-310-70256-9
ISBN-13: 978-0-310-70256-6
(Companion Nonfiction to *Rough and Rugged Lily*)
*The Year 'Round Holiday Book* will help you celebrate traditional holidays with not only fun and pizzazz, but with deeper meaning as well.

### Lily Speaks! (Book Ten)

Softcover • ISBN-10: 0-310-70262-3
ISBN-13: 978-0-310-70262-7

Lily enters the big speech contest at school and learns the up and downsides of competition through her pain and disappointment, as well as the surprise benefits, and how God heals jealousy, envy, and self-doubt.

### The Values & Virtues Book

Softcover • ISBN-10: 0-310-70257-7
ISBN-13: 978-0-310-70257-3
(Companion Nonfiction to *Lily Speaks!*)
*The Values & Virtues Book* offers you tips and skills for improving your study habits, sportsmanship, relationships, and every area of your life.

*Available now at your local bookstore!*

**zonderkidz**

## Horse Crazy Lily (Book Eleven)

Softcover • ISBN-10: 0-310-70263-1
ISBN-13: 978-0-310-70263-4

Lily's in love! With horses?! Back in the "saddle" for another exciting adventure,
Lily's gone western and feels she's destined to be the next famous cowgirl.

## The Fun-Finder Book

Softcover • ISBN-10: 0-310-70258-5
ISBN-13: 978-0-310-70258-0
(Companion Nonfiction to *Horse Crazy Lily*)

*The Fun-Finder Book* is designed to help you find out what you like so that you can
develop your own just-for-you hobby. And if you just can't figure it out, a self-quiz
helps you recognize your likes and dislikes as you discover your God-given talent.

## Lily's Church Camp Adventure (Book Twelve)

Softcover • ISBN-10: 0-310-70264-X
ISBN-13: 978-0-310-70264-1

Lily learns a real lesson about the essential habits of the heart
when she and the Girlz attend Camp Galilee.

## The Walk-the-Walk Book

Softcover • ISBN-10: 0-310-70259-3
ISBN-13: 978-0-310-70259-7
(Companion Nonfiction to *Lily's Church Camp Adventure*)

Every young girl needs the training that develops positive and lifelong spiritual
habits. Prayer, Bible study, devotion, simplicity, confession, worship, and celebration
are foundational spiritual disciplines to help you "walk-the-walk."

## Lily's in London?! (Book Thirteen)

Softcover • ISBN-10: 0-310-70554-1
ISBN-13: 978-0-310-70554-3

Lily's London adventures strengthen her relationship with God as she realizes, more
than ever, there are many possibilities for walking her spiritual path in Christ.

## Lily's Passport to Paris (Book Fourteen)

Softcover • ISBN-10: 0-310-70555-X
ISBN-13: 978-0-310-70555-0

Lily visits Paris and meets Christophe, an orphan boy at the mission where her
mom is working. While helping Christophe to understand who God is, Lily finally
discovers her own mission. This last book in the series also includes a letter from
Nancy Rue, which tells what happens to the characters after the series ends, and
introduces the character of Sophie LaCroix from the Faithgirlz! Sophie Series.

*Available now at your local bookstore!*

**zonderkidz**

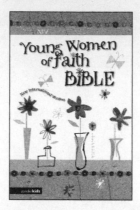

## NIV Young Women of Faith Bible

General Editor: Susie Shellenberger

Hardcover • ISBN-10: 0-310-91394-2
ISBN-13: 978-0-310-91394-8

Softcover • ISBN-10: 0-310-70278-X
ISBN-13: 978-0-310-70278-8

Now there is a study Bible designed especially for
girls ages 8 to 12. Created to develop a habit of studying God's
Word in young girls, the *NIV Young Women of Faith Bible* is full of
cool, fun to read in-text features that are not only interesting, but
provide insight. It has 52 weekly studies thematically tied to the
*NIV Women of Faith Study Bible* to encourage a special time of
study for mothers and daughters to share in God's Word.

### *Available now at your local bookstore!*

We want to hear from you. Please send your comments
about this book to us in care of zreview@zondervan.com. Thank you.

Grand Rapids, MI 49530
www.zonderkidz.com

**ZONDERVAN**.com/
**AUTHORTRACKER**
*follow your favorite authors*